KT-465-896

C014599210

ITA NUOVA

VITA NUOVA

Magdalen Nabb

WINDSOR
PARAGON

First published 2008
by William Heinemann
This Large Print edition published 2009
by BBC Audiobooks Ltd
by arrangement with
The Random House Group Ltd

Hardcover ISBN: 978 1 408 42879 5
Softcover   ISBN: 978 1 408 42880 1

Copyright © Magdalen Nabb and Diogenes Verlag
AG Zurich, 2008

Magdalen Nabb has asserted her right under the
Copyright, Designs and Patents Act, 1988, to be
identified as the author of this work

All rights reserved.

British Library Cataloguing in Publication Data available

HAMPSHIRE COUNTY LIBRARY

F

CO14599210

9781408428801

Printed and bound in Great Britain by
CPI Antony Rowe, Chippenham and Eastbourne

One

The marshal stood near the edge of the swimming pool, his eyes sheltered behind dark glasses from the glare of the low sun. A big yellow leaf lay still on the blue water. There was a scattering of wet leaves on the grass under his black shoes. The damp warmth made it seem like September, but the date on the notes in his top pocket was August 19. He turned his back on the pool and the stone tower standing on the other side of it. He looked down. No sound reached him up here, though the red roofs and marble towers of Florence lay below him. Normally you'd hear the muted drone of traffic. Of course, the city was pretty empty except for tourists. The pool had been built right on the brow of the hill, and no doubt you'd be able to raise your head from the water and see the dome and bell tower below an endless blue sky. Very nice. He didn't care for being in cold water himself, no matter how hot it got. He didn't care for this place at all, if he had to be honest, but there was no denying it was pretty fancy. He just didn't like it . . . this silence, the unshaded glare. He turned back and stared across the water at the tower. At the foot of it, two cream-coloured deck chairs faced the pool and a cream-coloured umbrella shaded a table and canvas chairs.

Shouldn't there be a nice orchard there, or maybe a vineyard, instead of the open blue glitter of a pool? The climbing sun burned his shoulder through his blue shirt. He stepped back, seeking shade.

1

Of the two women, it had been the young, pretty one who cried louder, roaring, hysterical, tears pouring down her cheeks, soaked tissues clutched in her hand. The mother was silent. Too stunned, perhaps. Sitting there on an upright chair in the kitchen, her face flushed and her eyes looking glazed rather than tearful, beads of sweat breaking at her temples. She made no move to comfort her daughter. She made no move at all. The kitchen was very big and full of fancy new equipment, but it was in a basement with windows set high and the marshal had found it oppressive. With the excuse of needing to meet the prosecutor on his arrival, he had been relieved to come back outside. The garden was as still and quiet as the water of the pool. One of the big yellow leaves floated down and stuck to the epaulette of his shirt. He brushed it off. He already felt too hot. If only it were really September. For a second his stomach tightened at the thought that the pleasant smell of fallen leaves would, from now on, call up the thick, sour smell of fresh entrails. That was ridiculous. For one thing, the chlorinated pool lay between him and the open doors at the base of the tower, and the dead woman was up on the second floor. The smell couldn't possibly be reaching him. Even so, he kept his breathing shallow. It was still in his nostrils. He could go back to the kitchen, but that feeling of oppression, or perhaps some undefined smell in there, too, made him reluctant. Nothing you could put your finger on. These people had money, a lot of money. The father was in a private clinic, his elder daughter dead, presumed murdered, a grandson, orphaned now, the other daughter weeping louder and louder, and no sign

2

of the prosecutor's car—what was taking him so long? No matter how far away he lived, there was no traffic in August. The marshal walked around the pool and turned the corner of the rough stone tower to return to the studded main doors of the villa, one of those fortified country houses from centuries ago, severe stone buildings with bars at the windows and military crenellations. His big shaded eyes took in everything along the way. The two family cars, a Mercedes convertible and a black Mini, were parked on the gravel in the shade of a big tree. The main gates were big and the perimeter wall high, but it would be easy enough to get in. He'd already taken a look behind the house and the gardens beyond that, and seen a bulldozer moving earth, digging out another swimming pool by the look of it. It was silent now. The carabinieri the captain had sent up had stopped the work. He had spotted the corner of a broken roof, low down on the hillside within the wall. A peasant's cottage. There was sure to be a door in the wall there and a cart track where, in the past, farm produce would have been taken down to Florence in trouble-free times—which didn't seem to have been frequent, from what he'd heard over his years here. The main doors had a sculpted stone coat of arms above them. It wasn't one he recognized and, anyway, it was almost worn away. He went inside and removed his hat and sunglasses. Still that crying, a bit quieter now, interspersed with low murmurs. A smooth, new grey stone floor, a modern wrought-iron railing, smooth, grey stairs leading down to the kitchen. Rich people always mean trouble. Everything depended on which prosecutor took the case. At

3

the sound of his heavy tread descending the staircase, the crying grew louder.

* * *

As it turned out, it was another hour before the prosecutor turned up. When he did, deeply tanned, white-linen-suited, paunch under a fine striped shirt, the marshal's heart sank. Fulvio De Vita. No doubt, the prosecutor was equally dismayed at the sight of the marshal's dark bulk standing in his path. They shook hands. He was a little breathless. You'd think he'd come here at breakneck speed!

'Guarnaccia, yes. I remember . . .'

And so do I, the marshal thought. Particularly the first time he had had to work with him. That case had been in August, too. A clear case of suicide, the prosecutor had decided, anxious to leave for his holidays. Of course, that murder victim had been poor and unimportant. All the stops would be pulled out for this one.

* * *

'Excuse me . . .'

They were on the second-floor landing of the tower and stood back now to let a young carabiniere with a video camera start work. The marshal's big eyes followed him. The cameraman closed in on the shell cases encircled in white chalk on the worn red tiles, then stepped inside, filming everything, detail by detail. So much more efficient than the human eye. The marshal himself had picked his way through the living room to where, beyond an open door, the body lay prone beside the bed. He had gone to check for signs of life, although, given the sloppy trail she had left as she dragged herself away from the door all the way through towards the bedside telephone, there was little chance of finding any. She hadn't made it to the phone. Her arm was stretched out in front of her, her hand touching the sculpted leg of the bedside table, but a bullet in the back of the head had stopped her. Perhaps she had grabbed at the leg. A photograph in a silver frame lay smashed on the shiny rug.

'Can we roll her?'

The cameraman stood back, and two technicians in hooded white overalls rolled the body over.

The cameraman called back to the prosecutor, 'Must be at least four or five bullets to the abdomen.'

'How much did the sister mess up the scene, Marshal?'

'She didn't. She said she ran away as soon as she saw the body from the doorway.'

'Without even checking if her sister was dead?'

'So she said.'

'You think she's telling the truth?'

'Yes. She didn't tread any blood outside. That would have been difficult.'

'Hmm. We don't know if anything was stolen, then.'

'No . . . though there's no sign of the place being ransacked.'

'No need for professionals to ransack a place. Robberies in villas like this one are well planned and often commissioned. They can be after one piece.'

5

'Yes . . .'

'But?' The prosecutor shot an aggressive look at him.

'But,' a long time had passed since the suicide that wasn't—and, besides, the marshal had been right, hadn't he? 'They don't usually leave this sort of thing behind them . . .'

'This sort of thing' was the body now being lifted into a metal coffin. A soft white robe hanging open, fat, bare legs. Blond hair swinging loose.

The prosecutor nodded his permission and they stood back again as the coffin was carried out.

'Professor Forli's assistant . . .' he felt for the notebook in the breast pocket of his blue shirt, 'gave me a time of death, judging from body temperature . . . around nine A.M. No rigor, no permanent lividity. He waited as long as—'

'Yes, yes. Thank you. Once I have his full report—what are the family members saying?'

The marshal turned back a page.

'The sister, Silvana Paoletti, lives in the main part of the villa with her parents. She came to collect her nephew, Piero, aged three, to take him to summer school at 8:15 because his mother, the victim, had to work. She drove him there, did a few errands in town, drove back and came up here to her sister's rooms in the tower, saw the body and ran away.'

'What made her call you, rather than calling an emergency number?'

'She didn't. She ran out into the road screaming and was seen from the house opposite. The woman who saw her was watering the garden, and she took her inside and called me because she knows me. That was at ten thirty-seven. Then she

6

came back with the sister and waited with her until I arrived because she was in such a state. She didn't come up here.'

'And who is this woman who knows you?' He summed up the marshal's probable acquaintance with a swift head-to-toe glance. 'Does she work at the house across the road?'

The house across the road was smaller than this place and probably built little more than a century ago, but it was a pretty grand house even so.

'No, she doesn't work there . . .' The marshal tucked his notebook back in his pocket and buttoned it. 'She's the owner.' He didn't explain that they knew each other because he'd helped out when her son wanted to do his national service in the carabinieri. He was a bit ashamed of himself. He didn't dine out with the people who lived on this most expensive of roads overlooking Florence. He didn't dine out with anybody. His heart sank at the thought of the evening ahead of him.

'And the mother?'

'She seems to be in a state of shock. Her husband's in hospital after a little stroke, so this coming on top . . . in any case, she was sound asleep when her daughter came back with the neighbour and went to tell her what had happened. She was still very dazed when I arrived. I could try to talk to her again tomorrow.'

'Perhaps . . . or it might be better if I spoke to her—I imagine that, in any case, you have your station to run—Palazzo Pitti, isn't it?'

'Yes.'

'I'll see her tomorrow morning, then. No point in your wasting your time running around unnecessarily. You say there's no husband, but I want the man in the victim's life found—father of the child, boyfriend, whoever she was seeing. Can't keep that sort of thing a secret. Somebody will know. Concentrate on that.'

'Of course—and, in any case, Lorenzini, my second-in-command, will be back from holiday shortly, so there should be no problem with—'

'Right . . .' The prosecutor was staring into the room where two technicians were still working, one picking through the stuff on the floor with tweezers of some sort, the other examining the sill of an open window. He didn't seem to be following their work, just staring, thoughtful. A frown creased his forehead. The tops of two cypress trees were still as sentries against the sky beyond the window. No breath of air entered the big bedroom. Only that one window was open. The morning sun, very hot now, lit the tumbled white bed, sprayed with a fine mist of red down one side. Doors to the bathroom and the child's bedroom stood open. The prosecutor's gaze remained fixed, absent. The marshal could well imagine that he might be deciding to get somebody else on the case. He had no illusions about this man's opinion of him. He knew it only too well after hearing the prosecutor's raised voice that time after leaving his office, all those years ago.

'The blank incomprehension of the man!'

Well, he was no great hand at talking and this prosecutor wasn't the first to get exasperated with him. Wouldn't be the last, either. And if he did get somebody else to take over, that was all to the good. The marshal was in a morose vein, as it was, and in no mood for treading around rich people who could cause him trouble.

8

'Good.' The prosecutor seemed to have come to some sort of decision. He picked up the briefcase at his feet and clapped his other hand on the marshal's shoulder. 'Right! So find the boyfriend—and bring the sister up here, once these people have finished, to check whether anything's been stolen. Come and see me tomorrow and bring me your report.' He shook hands and, all of a sudden, a dazzling white smile flashed across the suntan, which alarmed the marshal more than his anger had once done. What did it mean?

You shouldn't judge people hastily, of course. Maybe he'd mellowed over the years. Fellow seemed to have too many teeth, though. And his hair was dyed.

*   *   *

'And besides, I can't do with men who smell like a perfume shop—I know you're going to say I'm old-fashioned. Well, I *am* old-fashioned! Where the devil . . .' He was opening cupboard doors and slamming them shut without looking inside them properly, so he didn't find what he was looking for. 'Oh, Teresa!'

He stood still in the middle of the kitchen, having run out of cupboard doors to bang.

'And don't start on about men not being able to find things! If things were put in their proper place, they wouldn't have to be found, they'd be there!'

The phone rang. Now where . . . damn. He'd left the portable phone on the bed when he went to shower, in case she . . .

9

He went in the bedroom and picked the phone up but didn't sit down on the bed. Bad temper kept him standing rigid.

'Hello!'

'Salva? Are you all right?'

'No, I'm not all right. I thought you said you'd done the shopping before you left. The salt jar's empty.'

'Well, fill it.'

'How can I fill it if there's no salt?'

'In the cupboard to the left of the hood of the cooker, bottom shelf. Listen, Salva—I forgot to ask you last night—did you follow up on that flat Captain Maestrangelo told you about?'

'I haven't had time to be bothering with flats!'

'Oh, Salva, you said yourself things are quiet in August, that it's the best time to get things done. And don't shout.'

'I'm not shouting!' But he lowered his voice a bit. 'We'll talk about it when you get home.'

'But Captain Maestrangelo said we should get on to it right away.'

'There's no point if you're not here. What's the use of me looking at it, if then you don't like it?'

'You could get an idea, tell me about it, ask for the plans, show you're interested—besides, it's not a question of liking or not liking, it's whether or not it's a good investment. You could talk to the bank about how big a mortgage we could get.'

'No, no. It's August. The manager's on holiday.'

'The bank manager took his holiday in June. In the Caribbean, if you're interested. He wanted to give his wife a special holiday after that operation she had. He said you should just ring him, any day you're free, and he'll make himself available.'

'There is no day when I'm free. I've got a big case on.'

'In August?'

'Yes. In August. Not everybody's off at the seaside, taking it easy.'

'You always say there's nothing but small break-ins in empty houses in August. Aren't all the big criminals on holiday?'

'No, they're not. And it's not a break-in, it's—'

'Don't you want to know how Nunziata is?'

'How is she?'

'She's cheered up, that's the main thing.'

'That's because she's got you there.'

'Come on, now, Salva! Don't put that tragic voice on. You survived when I was down here looking after your mother.'

'I was younger then.'

'Really, the best thing for her is having the boys here. Totò said to her yesterday that she's his absolutely favourite auntie. And he really meant it, too. You should have seen her face.'

'She's his only auntie.'

'He said that, too! Right away, when he realized. You know Totò. He always makes her laugh. Oh— and the good news is that they're going to operate on Monday. She doesn't have to wait until September like we thought. Of course, these things have to be caught right away.'

'You'll be back sooner, then?'

'I don't know. It depends on whether she needs therapy afterwards.'

'Couldn't she come up here for that? What about school starting?'

'We'll see.'

'Don't say "we'll see"! That's what you say to the

11

boys!'

'It's also what the doctors are saying to Nunziata. Have you eaten?'

'What's that got to do with anything?'

'You know you get bad-tempered when you're hungry.'

'I'm not bad-tempered! And I would have eaten by now if I could have found the salt!'

'Oh, I knew there was something else I wanted to tell you. Listen . . .'

He listened, holding the receiver clamped to his ear so hard that it hurt, trying to get closer to her warming voice, not following a word of it.

'Concetto, the postman—you remember him— the flat above the grocer's at the corner of the piazza. His sister worked at the same place as Nunziata, but she left when she got pregnant with her second and then her husband was killed right away in that accident—now what was her second husband's name? It'll come to me in a minute— what was I telling you? Concetto, that's right. So, anyway, his mother was always trying to get him married off, never thinking . . . well, now she knows and she's more pleased than anything—I think she thinks she can keep him for herself, so she doesn't know the full story yet . . .

'So, I've said they can go, but they go together—I don't want Totò going out on his own and I've said so . . .

'Oh, and there's an Alberto Sordi film on at nine o'clock—that'll cheer you up . . .'

Nine o'clock. Well, he'd missed the beginning, but he knew it by heart anyway. Spaghetti or penne? Spaghetti, definitely spaghetti. He laid his solitary place at the kitchen table but without that

12

anxious loneliness in the pit of his stomach that he feared and hated. He could still feel his ear where the receiver had been pressed against it, still feel the warmth of her voice flowing through him. A big bowl of pasta and a glass of red would be good, and Alberto Sordi would take over after that. The evening had a shape now. He closed the window in spite of the boiling pan. He wanted to shut out the sawing of the cicadas out in the darkness of the Boboli Gardens. The sound made him lonely.

He wasn't one of those men who couldn't cope. He could cope all too well, that was the trouble. Years of it, when Teresa was still down in Syracuse looking after his sick mother and he had been posted to Florence. They'd had such plans and then, the stroke that had left her bedridden . . . long, lonely years. The rich man in the hospital had been luckier. Very slight, they said, a tiny haemorrhage. Have to watch his blood pressure, then. His own was all right, so far. Just his weight that—had to concentrate on the case. Hunger is a distraction. Just don't overdo it, Teresa always said.

Mm . . . that was so good, though he said it himself. Of course, she had made the tomato sauce . . . he was going to have just a bit of butter on it, too. He shouldn't, but he had to keep his energy *and* his spirits up if he wanted to work efficiently. This might be a delicate case and, anyway, it was a difficult time for him, being alone. It was Teresa who looked after his dieting.

'There's nothing fattening in any of these meals, so as long as you don't overdo it with bread . . . and remember to take them out of the freezer the night before . . .'

13

Well, he'd forgotten. He had other things to think about, so, until she came home . . .

It had been difficult for Teresa, too, with a sick mother-in-law to care for and no husband to comfort her—but at least she hadn't been on her own. She'd had the children and his sister Nunziata. It took both of them just to turn her in the bed . . .

The loneliness of sitting here, eating by himself, night after night, like now.

Bit more cheese. He liked it freshly grated, didn't like it sitting in a bowl in the fridge for days, the way some people did, and some restaurants, too. It went sour. He liked chewing the basil leaves in his sauce, too, and he always told Teresa to leave them whole. The boys picked them out and left them, and Teresa—

Damn! He should have told her about the prosecutor's sudden affability. Women are better at understanding that sort of thing. Could be, of course, that in the end he'd remembered that the marshal had been right about that so-called suicide. No, no . . . as if he'd care either way, and even if he had cared, he'd have forgotten by now. It was years ago. No chance of calling this one a suicide. Wouldn't do, anyway. Rich families don't like it.

Chewing over the morning's events, one phrase came to the surface: Robberies in villas like this one . . .

'No, no . . .' Bit of bread—only a small piece. Had to mop up the last traces of sauce.

He got up from the table and washed his bowl, fork, and glass and the big pan. There was still some sauce in the small one, so he put it in the

14

fridge.

'No.' Had the family whose coat of arms was above the doors still been in residence, that might have been true. Paintings and so on. But no, he'd seen backstage before the prosecutor arrived. The man lying in the private clinic might have been rich enough to buy the villa, but all that building work going on behind and the second swimming pool, hardly the style of a noble Florentine family. He'd talked to the builders—well, one of them, anyway, since the others didn't speak Italian. They were all from Rumania, apart from one Moroccan, and they were working right through August, dividing the colonnade and outbuildings behind the villa into three luxury flats with a communal garden and pool. Two of them had already been sold. People from Milan, the builder said. And then there was that kitchen full of all the latest expensive equipment . . . a far cry from the Florentine nobility, that was. From what little he'd seen of those people, they counted how many matches their servants used. No. No . . .

He glanced around his own tidy kitchen, switched the light off, and went back to his office where the two or three notes he'd taken that morning lay on his desk ready to be worked up into a scene-of-the-crime report. It was a simple enough job—or it used to be, until the arrival of That Thing.

'That Thing,' as he always referred to it, was the personal computer sitting in the middle of his desk. He'd avoided it as long as he could, but, these days, all information had to be computerized and so available throughout the country. Even the daily orders to which only he had the password. All

15

very efficient, of course. He sighed as he switched the wretched Thing on and waited. It was *so slow.* He'd have had a good half of his report typed with two fingers by now, but instead here he was listening to tiddly bits of music while it sent up pretty pictures, offered him a dozen things he didn't want, asked him for the same old information and then—just when he thought he could get started—popped up with a suggestion that it could run an anti-virus check.

'No-o!' Blast the thing. Still, might as well say yes. He could be having a think about things . . .

The mother and daughter, for instance. The daughter was what? He looked at the date of birth on his notes . . . twenty-five. Pretty, you could tell, despite the blotched face and the tears. Slim, with dark hair in a long plait behind. No makeup, though he'd noticed tiny traces of eye makeup on the wet tissues that were all over the enormous glass table, so she must use it sometimes. Been out the night before, perhaps. She wore a simple flowery summer frock that, together with the plait, made her look like a little girl. The crying, too, of course. There were so many ways of crying and, in his job, the marshal had heard a lot of them. Most adults smothered their crying, tried to force it back, but this young woman was roaring, loud and unashamed, for help and comfort. The marshal's instinct had been to place a big soothing hand on her head, as he did with his own children, but these days you had to be careful, so he'd looked at the mother. No response at all. Poor woman. Hardly any wonder she was shocked into silence. She was a blonde, like her dead daughter, bleached now, mixed with the grey, but you could

16

tell by her pale blue eyes. Fifty-one . . . looked older but, then, she was overweight. Born in the Alto Adige and given that her name was German—Anna Wertmuller—she would be German-speaking. Funny, that . . . there was little love lost between Italian and German speakers up there, and you wouldn't expect her to have moved down here. Well, he didn't know a lot about it and today had certainly not been the time to ask. When he'd tried to talk to her, she had only stared up at him like a frightened child might, as though she were waiting for him to tell her what to do. What could he tell her? The only thing he could think of was to try to interrupt the daughter's crying and suggest she give her mother a drop of something.

'*She doesn't drink!*' The phrase had somehow been howled without interrupting the crying at all.

He ought to try to talk to them both tomorrow, whatever the prosecutor said. For a long time, he pictured the two of them in that huge kitchen he so disliked. Those high, barred windows, a closed door that presumably led to servants' quarters. A place that size would be a lot of work—but what sort of newfangled idea was it to make a kitchen in the cellar? It was really a wine cellar, with a vaulted ceiling. The faintest trace of a smell that came and went . . . what was it? Each time he'd tried to identify it, it escaped him. Something innocuous, maybe, but connected with an unpleasant memory? The wet tissues she kept squeezing had a light perfume, but it surely couldn't be that. Short, unvarnished nails . . .

The dead woman . . . he looked at his notes again. Daniela. Older than her sister . . . twenty-seven. Single mother . . . well, the prosecutor was

17

right about that, anyway, the man in her life being the prime suspect, as always. He'd need the men the captain had sent him again tomorrow. They had searched the tower, and the grounds immediately below it, all day and found no weapon. That whole area where there was building going on remained to be searched. It had to be done, though the marshal was pretty sure they wouldn't find anything. Why would he leave it behind? Somebody cool enough to put that bullet in the back of his victim's head . . . anyone in a panic would have fled as soon as she hit the floor. Captain Maestrangelo had agreed with him about that when they'd talked on the phone that evening.

'*A very cool customer. Especially when you think how long she must have taken to drag herself through the living room and into the bedroom in that condition. And he stood there at the door, watching—there were no shell cases inside the flat?*'

'*No.*'

'*Very sure of himself. Sure of his aim, too. And no trace of him in the room, I imagine.*'

'*It doesn't look like it.*'

'*Sounds professional. What do you think?*'

'*Well . . .*'

'*You don't think so.*'

'*No, I'm sure you're right. Only . . . to stand there watching . . . he could have finished her off right away, couldn't he? To watch that . . . you'd have to really hate somebody—not that that rules out . . . I'm not saying you're not right, of course.*'

'*You were on the spot, Guarnaccia, and your instincts are always sound—which leaves us with a professional with a personal grudge. Well, it happens, of course.*'

'*Yes. But this was a young mother, leading a very quiet life, unless . . .*'

'*Unless things aren't what they seem?*'

'*Yes. I'll find out.*'

The captain had made no comment on the prosecutor assigned to the case. Just the briefest silence before saying, '*I'm sure you'll be all right.*'

The captain was the soul of discretion—the captain . . . damn! If he'd thought of it, he could have asked about the flat then—but as if he had time to be looking at flats now! What was the point anyway, on his own? It was true that they'd been putting it off for years and that it had to be done. You went on spending your income, house prices rose and rose and come the day you retired . . . it was the right thing to do. Buy something, rent it out, a good investment, keep up with the market . . . no! Not without Teresa. And now he had this case on his hands, so that was that.

As if to prove how busy he was, he placed his big hands on the keyboard and found himself staring into a blank dark screen. If the blasted thing hadn't finished fiddling around playing music, checking viruses and God knows what and then, for want of attention, switched itself off!

'If I've said it once, I've said it a hundred times!' he bellowed at Lorenzini, only to be met with another blank silence. Lorenzini, his second in command, was still at the seaside with his family.

'Well, I've had enough!' He shut the lid of That Thing and closed up his office. It would have to be typed first thing in the morning, because he was going to catch the rest of that film and go to bed. And he would have done just that if it hadn't been almost midnight and the film long over. He

19

switched on the mosquito killer and stared at the satin-smooth emptiness of the bed, his huge eyes mournful.

Two

The builder wasn't happy. He wasn't happy at all.

'And if the boss comes?'

'It's not your fault. Prosecutor's orders. You'd do better to go home, all of you, until we've finished.'

'We're paid by the hour, you know, and we lost all but the first couple of hours yesterday. He's always late paying us, as it is, and this'll give him another excuse at the end of this month, you'll see.'

None of the others spoke; they kept their heads down. The marshal assumed that all of them, with the exception of this one man, Cristiano, a legal immigrant from Rumania who spoke Italian, were without papers. The captain's men had searched their toolbags yesterday and they had all looked scared.

'I'm sorry, but there's nothing I can do . . .' The marshal felt sorry for them, but the search was clearly going to take at least another full day. 'You're absolutely sure in your own mind that none of them saw a stranger around yesterday morning? That they're not just saying they didn't because they're frightened of being involved? You did explain to them that I'm not interested in whether they have papers or not?'

'I told them that this is about a murder, not about their situation. They'd say if they knew

20

anything. They trust me.'

The marshal believed him. Cristiano was a big man like himself, calm and solid and not frightened at all.

'Besides, I was here before eight, and you can see for yourself how quiet it is round here. You can hear a leaf fall, let alone a car arriving, or even footsteps on the gravel driveways.'

'And that thing?' The cement mixer, switched off now. 'Don't you start mixing cement first thing— and what about the bulldozer that was working when I arrived?'

'That's true . . . he finished yesterday morning and he was taking it away when you people arrived and stopped him. They searched him, too, and took his name and address. He was none too pleased. The boss'll be furious, as well, because every day it stays here it will have to be paid for.'

'It can go today. And this cement mixer?'

'You're right. It was going from eight until when you arrived . . . I didn't think . . .'

'No. Well, you'd likely have heard the shots, otherwise, and the woman who ran out screaming.'

'You're right . . . sorry.'

'Don't worry. We none of us notice the noises that are always there.'

Of course, the man could, in theory, have been with her all night, but there was no trace of sexual activity up to now, and he had shot her from outside the door . . .

'What about tomorrow, then? Can we work?'

'It should be all right. Give me your number, just in case. If we haven't finished, I'll let you know tonight.'

'Thanks.'

The important thing, for the marshal, was that they had all turned up for work this morning. Frightened as they were, any idea of a messed-up attempted robbery by one of them, unlikely as it was, faded to nothing.

The marshal started to walk away, treading on planks laid over churned-up yellowish earth. This must have been a wonderful place once. Probably the only building on this wooded hill that was now scarred all over with a rash of fancy houses and bright blue swimming pools. He stopped, hearing a fuss behind him, a voice raised in protest. He turned to look.

One of the builders, young, dark-haired, was gesticulating and shouting at Cristiano. His desperation sounded very real and, as the marshal walked back, he saw the man wave a piece of paper in Cristiano's face. He fell silent and turned away when he saw the marshal coming.

'What's going on?'

'Nothing, Marshal, nothing—I mean to say, nothing to do with your business. It's just that we didn't get paid at the end of July—not properly paid, anyway. I had a bit of a showdown with the boss, and he did give us something but nowhere near what he owes us, so you see why I'm not happy about sending them home. I've got a bit put by, I'm used to this, but Milo's desperate. We were hoping the boss would come by today like he promised and give us a bit of cash.'

'And what's on that paper he was waving?'

'Nothing, it's just—'

'Tell him to give it to me.'

Cristiano murmured something to the other man, who handed over the bit of paper. His face

22

was red. The marshal couldn't read it, but he could see it was a list and he recognized the brand name of some baby food.

'It's just a shopping list, that's all. His wife gave it to him this morning. Mostly baby food and stuff. Fifteen euros would have covered it and we thought that today, the boss . . . he was hoping to go to the supermarket after work, but he hasn't a bean. If he turns up at home at this time, with his day's work lost and empty-handed . . .'

Milo was bending over, packing his toolbox. His face was hidden but his hands were trembling. The marshal drew Cristiano aside, took a couple of notes from his pocket and murmured, 'Tell him to do his shopping. I'm going to be around for a while, so he can pay me back later and, in the meantime, give me your boss's number—I'll have a word with him, tell him I've got my eye on his business and don't want to hear any complaints about him. He'll pay up tomorrow, and he'll regularize their status, too, you'll see.'

'Thanks, Marshal.'

'It's an ill wind, as they say . . .'

The captain's men seemed to be all down in the newly dug swimming-pool hole. They were working in silence. One of them saw him and waved a negative. They wouldn't find anything with their metal detectors except junk. The marshal walked on. There had been thunder during the night and, judging by the wet lawns and bushes, some rain. Now the sky was innocent and blue, the birds chirping. Please, God, let the sister have stopped crying. He walked under an archway, through the wing that was being converted. He guessed it had once been the stabling and carriage

23

house, outbuildings of various kinds. He kept close to the walls, where the gravel path was shaded by wooden eaves, and returned to the main part of the house. The garden with its low, geometrical box hedging was on a lower terrace cut into the hillside. Vineyards and an olive grove below and a bit of pasture. Then the perimeter wall. These flower beds looked exhausted and messy after weeks of relentless heat and stagnation. The marshal felt the same. Whatever all that fuzzy flowery stuff confined by the low hedges was, it was dead or dying, and last night's bit of rain had only helped the weeds. Needed some attention. No sign of a gardener. The studded doors stood open and he could see along the flagged carriageway and out of the front doors that he'd used yesterday. He felt someone was watching him. From inside the passage . . . ? No. After that . . . he walked on a bit, his footsteps loud on the gravel, then stopped. That prickling sensation . . . but where . . . ? Perhaps there was a gardener, after all, and he looked down to his right, scanning the area, but there was no possible place to watch from in that glaring, geometrical emptiness. Turning his gaze straight ahead, he walked forward again and knew for certain that something pale flickered low down to his left. The long barred windows of the kitchen near his feet—or, no, he'd already passed those, must be the other rooms at that level. There had been a door to what would be some sort of servants' quarters, he remembered. Somebody he still needed to talk to . . . only natural they should be curious. Could be scared, even, given what had happened. Somebody else without a work permit, no doubt. These days . . .

He walked on to the tower at the end. These oak doors, too, stood open. He'd sent a carabiniere up there with the sister to check for missing objects.

'And if she shows signs of bursting into tears, bring her down right away. This was never any robbery, and I want her in good enough shape to talk, understand?'

The ground floor of the tower was stone-flagged. A shower and a slatted wooden changing room had been built in one corner, and there was an enormous fridge which yesterday's search had revealed to be crammed with soft drinks and fruit. There was a long, marble-topped table at one side of the room, and deck chairs, beach umbrellas, and a lot of big toys on the other. So the room was servicing the swimming pool outside. The steep stone staircase looked pretty dangerous for a three-year-old to the marshal, and it was certainly hard work for him. As he climbed, he listened for sounds of crying but heard none. And as he listened, he thanked heaven he'd arranged to talk to the sister up here instead of going down to that kitchen again—must remember to ask . . . that flicker of a face watching him. Hadn't the sister said yesterday there was nobody in the house except herself and her mother? Sitting down there in that cellar-kitchen in this great place . . .

Thank goodness for the smooth stone banister. Far too high for a three-year-old . . .

And why would these rich people receive him in the kitchen, anyway? Some sort of insult, keeping him in his place? No, the prosecutor had gone down there, too, when he'd finally turned up.

'Uff!' The last flight.

The carabiniere was on the landing.

25

'She says there's nothing missing.'

'Was she all right when you took her into the bedroom?' The bed and the stained rug beside it had been covered with polythene sheeting.

'She seemed to be. I'll go down to help the others, unless you need me.'

'All right—no, wait. Go across the road to the neighbour who was here yesterday. Her name's Donati, Costanza Donati. Tell her I sent you and ask her if she's remembered anything else other than what she told me yesterday—which was nothing, but she was pretty agitated. Anybody going in or out of here by car or on foot, other than the people who live here, including the ones they never think to tell you about, postman, delivery, you know the form. Anybody hanging around in the last few days, and . . .' He drew the younger man away from the doorway and murmured, 'Ask if she ever saw the victim going in or out with a man.'

The carabiniere clattered off down the stone stairs. The marshal tapped on the open door.

'May I?'

She was sitting on a big, white covered sofa, intent on examining a box in her lap. A shaft of sunlight from the open window made red glints on her smooth dark head and glittered in the gold chain running through her fingers. The door that opened on the bedroom was closed now. The trail of stuff through this first room had been cleaned up after the forensics people had finished.

She looked up but didn't speak. She was wearing a dark blue T-shirt, a cotton skirt, and brown leather sandals. The marshal noticed that her long dark hair hung loose down her back today and

26

that, without the swollen red eyes, she was even prettier than he'd thought.

'What about the jewellery? You're sure there's nothing missing?'

She was twining the gold necklace round her fingers.

'It's all here.'

'You never know, your sister might have bought herself something nice, something valuable.'

'She couldn't have. She had no money.'

He stood looking down at her. Her long fingers were opening and closing on the necklace. It wasn't just a chain, it was wider and as delicately worked as lace and a jewelled cross hung from it. She could easily break it with her nervous hands. Still, at least she wasn't crying . . .

'No money at all? I suppose, this being your parents' house, she lived here for free and you told me yesterday she worked, that you drove the little boy to summer school yesterday because your sister had to work.' He spoke gently, chose his words, hoping to avoid another flood of tears.

'She's working on her doctoral thesis in Chemistry and she helps out in the registrar's office at the university sometimes at busy times. They're busy now because enrolments started in July but she only does a few hours a week. She had no money for buying jewellery.'

'What about a present from a boyfriend? A ring, even. They may have quarrelled and he took it away because the purchase could be traced, you see, perhaps through a credit card. Did she wear a ring?'

'No. Can I keep this? I want to keep it. Daddy gave it to her for her First Communion.'

Her face flushed on the instant she said it. Tears welled up.

'Of course. You want something to remember her by. You don't have to explain. Consider it yours, but just leave it here for the moment. It will no doubt all be yours once this investigation's over.'

'I don't want anything else.'

'You think about it later. I'm sure your sister would have wanted you to have them, or your mother, perhaps. They look like very nice pieces. Are those real diamonds there?'

'Of course they're real, and I don't want any of them! I'm not interested in jewellery!'

'Try not to get agitated. Breathe deeply.'

She did as she was told, lifting up her face, keeping her big dark eyes fixed on him, appealing for help.

'That's right. Deeply and slowly. I have to ask you questions, but there's no hurry. If you get too upset or tired, we'll stop and carry on tomorrow. All right?'

She nodded, her fingers still clutching the necklace, her gaze still fixed on him, thick dark lashes fringing the unblinking eyes . . .

'All right. Tell me a little about yourself.' The upsetting bits would have to be dealt with a bit at a time, at long intervals. 'You were looking after your little nephew yesterday. Does that mean you don't work? Keep breathing deeply. There's no hurry.'

'I'm all right. I'll be all right. I help Daddy in his office, but not full-time.'

The flush was fading, thank God.

'I see. What sort of office is it?'

'A staffing agency. We place people in jobs, domestic mostly, some secretarial.'

Obedient to his instructions, she was breathing deeply, very audibly.

'I see. So, if I needed a cook or a gardener, I'd come to you?'

'Yes.'

'At least, I would if I could afford it.'

'Our fees are no higher than anyone else's.'

'I'm sure they're not. I only meant I couldn't afford a cook or a gardener.' He smiled to indicate that he hadn't meant it seriously.

'Oh . . .' She did a fleeting imitation of his smile and the fixed stare returned.

'You're lucky to live in this beautiful place.' He didn't mean that seriously, either, because he wouldn't like to live in this sad old house whose roots were being torn up by bulldozers. So empty. Yet, behind her head, beyond the open window, was a perfect panorama of Florence below a serene summer sky.

Tread carefully, he warned himself. She looked as much like a frightened child as her mother did, but a rich family has expensive lawyers. This was a minefield. There had to be a man in this story . . .

'Do you mind if I sit down here?' He pulled up a sturdy-looking chair. The furniture in here was austere, solid stuff that looked as if it belonged in the stone watchtower, but the fine rugs and white chair coverings, the book-lined walls and the shaft of sunshine softened the effect. The marshal had an eye for solidity in chairs. Better not to loom over her, in any case. 'You don't mind?'

'No. But—do you have to wear those dark glasses? It bothers me.'

'I'm sorry. It's only because I have a bit of a problem with my eyes.'

'You weren't wearing them yesterday.'

'No. Down in the kitchen, no. Up here, the sunshine ...' She was observant enough, despite being upset, but that didn't mean she'd tell him what she observed. 'If you wouldn't mind just closing the shutters a little.'

She set the jewel case aside and got up to pull the brown shutters inwards at the open window.

'Thank you.' He slipped the sunglasses into the top pocket of his blue shirt. 'Is that better?' A good idea, anyway, he thought, as she sat down again. The shadowy room might be more conducive to a confidential talk. 'Your sister must have been very clever, judging by all the books in here. Were most of her friends from the university? I suppose she brought some of them home?'

'No. When she wasn't studying, she spent her time with me and with my parents and looking after Piero.'

'Of course. She must have been very busy.' Kept him a secret from the family, then. Somebody at the university was sure to know.

'What about Piero's father? Did you know him?'

'She would never tell us who it was.'

'But I expect you had suspicions? You would have known if she had a boyfriend, wouldn't you, even if you never met him?'

'No. She always kept secrets from us. Mummy sometimes called her The Lodger, because even though Daddy insists we all have supper together every evening and she took turns with me cooking it, she never really talked to us.'

30

'No? Well . . . chemistry, you said. They say scientists do live in their own world, that they're absent-minded.'

'She was like that when she was ten.'

'Showed early signs, then . . . You didn't think it might be a married man who was the father, and that was why she never talked about him or brought him home?'

Silence. Looking down at the necklace which she was winding more and more tightly round her fingers, she seemed to be giving the idea some thought.

'Maybe . . . ,' she said at last.

'And what about you? What did you study?'

'Music. I went to the conservatory. I was going to be a singer, but then I was seriously ill. I was in hospital for over a year and I had to give it up.'

'That's a pity. Do you still sing, though?'

She shrugged. 'Sometimes. My voice is still good, but I wanted to be a first-class professional. I'm not interested in being a talented amateur.'

'I can understand that.' Would she now become the family drudge, helping in the office, bringing up her sister's child, caring for her mother?

'Your father is going to be all right, you know that?' Something the prosecutor had checked on with the doctors before telling him the bad news. There was one advantage, then, in a case involving rich people. The prosecutor did some of the difficult jobs usually left to the marshal. 'And you know that there's a patrol car outside the gates, so you've no reason to be frightened. They'll be inside the grounds at night.'

'They weren't there this morning when I took Piero.'

31

'No, but they're there now and they'll stay. You may see some journalists out there, too. Just ignore them. They won't be allowed to bother you. I imagine you'll need to go out later to pick the little boy up.'

'I collect him at four. I haven't told him. He keeps asking me when she's coming back, and I don't know what to say to him.'

Her face flushed red again, her eyes glittered.

'Try to breathe quietly . . . ' Tears began to roll down her blotched cheeks, but she made no move to dry them, just continued to gaze at him. Having nothing else to offer her, he gave her his clean white handkerchief.

'Thank you. He's my responsibility now. I'll have to tell him sometime.'

'Yes, you'll have to tell him. The main thing is that he has you. I do think, though, that you need to calm down yourself before you can explain that she's not coming back. You can't do it when you're in this state. In the meantime, do you have any help here? Someone to watch the child if you have to be elsewhere? A housekeeper, a maid perhaps?' There hardly seemed to be any point in mentioning her mother as a possible help.

'There are two girls who work here. They don't live in, but Daddy phoned me last night and told me one of them should stay here now. She slept in the main house last night, but now that—now she's to sleep here in Daniela's bedroom so that Piero can stay in his own room next door. I have to stay with Mummy.'

'That sounds sensible, but you'll have to wait for the prosecutor to give his permission for anyone to use the tower. It may not be for a while yet.'

32

'Why, as I'm here now?'

'Yes. But you're not here alone. We needed your help to check that nothing was missing, and you've been very sensible, but now the doors will be sealed and you must all stay in the main house. Please don't worry. It's only until the investigation's over.' He was conscious of treating her as though she were a child or a delicate invalid, or perhaps, to be honest, more like a bomb that might explode in another paroxysm of hysterical tears. But she was drying her eyes and waiting quietly for his next question. A pigeon fluttered, trying to land on the windowsill, frustrated by finding the shutters pulled to. What had the technicians been checking there yesterday? Did they think the man had been secretly climbing up to the princess in the tower?

'Did your sister feed the birds?'

'No. I don't know. Maybe she did. I never came up here. She always brought Piero down to the car, and when she wasn't studying we spent the afternoons by the pool. Daddy was going to start teaching Piero to swim and now . . . and now . . .'

'He will teach him to swim. He will. You can't believe it now, I know, but life will go on. It does for us all. It will be all right.'

'No.' She said it in a low voice with a dreadful, black certainty and he saw her body hunch, curling in on itself as if rigid with pain. 'No, it won't. It'll never be all right, and he'll blame me.'

All of a sudden, the room was too dark. The gloom spared his eyes, but she needed sunshine. If she went to pieces, there'd be no witness in this case. This wouldn't do at all. He shouldn't have sent that carabiniere down, either. The last thing

33

he needed was for the prosecutor to arrive to talk to the mother and find he'd sent the daughter into a fit of hysterics. That would be the end of his affability.

'Why don't you open the shutters now? I'll sit out of the way of the strong light. I won't put my dark glasses on, don't worry.'

She stayed where she was, hunched and rigid, eyes fixed on the chain pulled tight between her reddening fingers. He got up and went behind the sofa to close the window. The only light came from the small bare windows of the landing and staircase. He had to get her out of here.

'I think we should go down. You're getting upset.'

'I want Daddy to come home! I can't manage by myself!'

'I'm sure he'll be home in a very few days, but he won't want to find you in this state. He's going to be all right, but he has been ill and he'll need your help, your comfort.'

'He won't! He'll blame me! I don't want him to come home!'

'Why should he blame you? You weren't even here—and if you had been, what could you have done against an armed man?'

'No, I wasn't here. I wasn't here . . . I was—do you want to know where I was? Trying on shoes! I didn't tell you that yesterday, did I? I forgot—no, I didn't . . . I was ashamed to tell you I was trying on shoes at Gucci. Yes. Trying on shoes when—when—Oh, God! Oh, God!' Her face was pale now.

'No, no, no. This won't do at all. It'll do no good to start blaming yourself. Breathe deeply.

34

Breathe.'

Thank heaven she responded to orders. He must get her downstairs and out into the open.

'Come with me now. We're going to go down and walk in the garden until you feel calmer.'

He went down the steep stairs in front of her, still afraid she might faint, sure she would follow him. When calm, she was docile enough.

Outside, slipping on his hat and dark glasses, he felt safer and was relieved to see the carabiniere he'd sent across the road coming towards them.

'Walk with us a moment and tell me how it went.'

'I'm afraid I've nothing to report, even the other matter you mentioned . . .' He glanced at the victim's sister in embarrassment.

'That's all right. I just thought we should take a look at the garden, get our bearings.'

The young carabiniere was confused. He was ingenuous and enthusiastic and clearly itching to get back to the search for the weapon with the other men, perhaps hoping he'd be the one to find it. It was easy to see he couldn't understand what the marshal wanted.

'We're going to search an empty cottage, Marshal, just inside the wall. There's a gate down there and a track. The lieutenant says somebody could have got in there easily and that—'

'Walk with us,' insisted the marshal, silencing the carabiniere. 'It's very pleasant here . . . A garden this size, now,' the marshal pretended to look about him, 'must be a lot of work. And a pool to look after, too.'

'Daddy likes doing that. There's a robot thing.'

'Ah, yes. I know what you mean. I think there's even one that mows grass by itself—does your

35

father like gardening, too? No, I suppose you have a gardener.'

'No.'

'And you're not interested in gardening yourself?'

'No.'

Not interested in this line of questioning either, that was evident. Not a flicker of reaction. If little Piero had been fathered by a sprightly young gardener, she didn't know about it.

'All these hedges to cut. And watering in this heat. So, who does it?'

'Contract gardeners cut the hedges, once a month. The watering system's automatic. We did have a man once . . .'

'How long ago was that?'

'I forget. A few years ago, but Daddy had to sack him.'

'Can you remember why?'

'I think because he was stealing. There was a quarrel, anyway. Daddy was furious with him, said he was ungrateful.'

'I see. Shall we go along here—this didn't used to be a vegetable garden, by any chance, did it?'

'I think so. Why?'

'Oh, no reason, just that I saw one like it once, divided up with these little hedges. Why should he have been grateful? The gardener.'

'Because he was an ex-prisoner and Daddy gave him a job as a favour.'

'I understand. Well, we have to consider anyone with a grudge against your father as under suspicion. I'll talk to him about it once he's home. What about the two girls you mentioned? I imagine they were here when . . . when you left with the little boy yesterday. I'll need to talk to them. You said yesterday you didn't see anybody around the villa or coming away in a car when you returned, but they might have noticed something. I didn't see them here yesterday.'

'Because they weren't here. I told you there was nobody here except Mummy and me. They don't come until lunchtime. They bring the shopping and prepare lunch. Then, in the afternoon, they do the housework and leave everything ready for supper. They usually leave about nine, only now Frida has to stay. Are we going down to the vineyard?'

'No, no . . . we'll turn back. The sun's hot and you have nothing on your head.'

'I never wear anything on my head.'

'Well, of course, you have lovely thick hair. Even so, you can't be too careful, eh, carabiniere?'

'What? Oh . . . no, Marshal.'

'Unusual hours. The two girls, I mean.'

'It's because of Mummy. She's not well and she always has trouble sleeping. She takes something for it and she never gets up until late.'

'Except yesterday, of course, when all the noise—but no, you said you woke her, didn't you? You understand that I'd rather not have to press her too much. She's very upset and, if you say she's not well, anyway—but I do need to know whether she heard anything.'

'She didn't. She couldn't have. I told you she takes sleeping pills and she wears earplugs as well. I didn't wake her, it was the woman across the road when she came back here with me. It took her a long time to wake Mummy at that hour.'

'Ah, yes. Signora Donati. Let's walk down this

37

path. The carabiniere here has just been chatting to her. Do you know her well?'

She didn't answer right away. Her gaze shifted away and up. He followed her glance. The tower. It was going to be a long time before she could look up there without that image coming back. It had been hard on her to expect her help today, but then who else was there to ask? Not the mother, that went without saying.

'I'm sorry. What did you ask me?'

'I was asking if you knew Signora Donati well.'

'Who is she?'

'The neighbour who helped you yesterday.'

'I don't know her at all.'

Of course not. How much easier it was to investigate a crime in the poorer parts of the old city where everybody knew everybody else's business.

'You went to her for help, though.'

'No, I didn't. I was just running away. I was frightened and he was out there and—and I was screaming . . . I've been thinking about what you asked me yesterday—I mean about whether I saw anybody . . .'

'You've remembered something?'

'I'm not sure. I just thought—I was upset and I couldn't remember anything clearly. I'll try . . .'

'The person you thought you saw, was it somebody you recognized? Don't be afraid to say. Even if you're mistaken and remember more clearly later, it's all right.'

'Is it?'

'Of course. I'm not writing anything down, am I? And the carabiniere here is not writing anything down, either, are you?'

'I—no. No.'

'After what you'd just seen, anybody would be confused and in a panic. If you take things calmly, it will all come back, bit by bit. We won't write anything down until you're quite sure.'

For a moment she remained silent. Their footsteps on the gravel seemed very loud in the silence. The marshal didn't insist, didn't prompt. She had said 'he was out there.' She wasn't seeing Signora Donati watering her flowers, she was seeing a man. But he mustn't suggest it. She seemed to him a bit too docile to be a good witness. Like so many people looking for a lifeline in their distress, she would probably be only too willing to say what she thought he wanted to hear.

*　　　*　　　*

'It was a man.'

'She actually said she saw a man? You didn't suggest it? Well, of course not, with your experience and know-how. Excellent!' The prosecutor, with his wide grin, really seemed pleased.

Fortunately, the shutters of his office in the Procura were closed against the sun and the desk lamp was on. The marshal always had an ample supply of folded white handkerchiefs, but he would not like his sun-sensitive eyes to start acting up here. Despite their newfound friendship, he didn't fancy having to wipe away his tears in front of this man. 'Experience and know-how . . .' Good Lord. Well, it made a change for the marshal to be receiving compliments, even if he hardly believed them. It would make life easier.

39

'I'm just thinking that if she said "he" like that, then what she was seeing in her head wasn't the neighbour watering her flowers. It was the man. I don't know if I'm making myself clear . . .'

'Perfectly. I couldn't agree more.'

The marshal was almost encouraged to go on. But the other images crowding his head were more difficult to get into focus. The slender figure with long dark hair, the exposed fat legs dropping into a metal coffin . . . well, married man or not, would you bring any boyfriend home if your sister were that good-looking? First-born children are always jealous—not Giovanni, though . . . adored Totò. Even so, it could have happened before, maybe with the father of the child. Silvana was twenty-five and single. Of course, these days women had careers, didn't marry so young as they used to. Not much of a career, ferrying a nephew around and working part-time in daddy's office. She'd been ill, of course, but so many women were sacrificed by the family. His own sister, Nunziata, would have been a candidate for that, and it was thanks to Teresa if she'd had any freedom at all after their mother . . .

The mother's face . . . was she all there? Was it just the sleeping pills?

'Hmph . . .' was all he said, looking at the photographs spread on the desk.

'Six bullets to the abdomen,' the prosecutor followed his glance. 'One to the back of the head. One missing.'

'One missing?'

'Eight shell cases—incidentally, bad news from ballistics. I don't have their report yet, but they've already told me we're talking Beretta 22 LR, shells

40

are Winchester.'

'Oh, dear . . .'

'Commonest gun in the country, used by every target shooter. Well, it's not the end of the world but it's certainly no help. People imagine ballistic evidence can provide cast-iron proof of a gun's identity, but you and I know that's far from the truth. Unless they come up with some extraordinary defect by way of a distinguishing trait, it's more difficult than telling identical twins apart.'

'Yes . . .' You and I . . . a newfound friend. Well, as long as it lasted . . .

'It's the man himself we need to find, anyway. Keep talking to the sister, get her to be more precise.'

'I'll be talking to the young lady again tomorrow. To the father, too, as soon as he gets home. Not that he can help us much with the event itself, but he might at least have some suspicions about his daughter's relationships and so on—the mother didn't have anything to say about that to you when you saw her this morning?'

'No. Not really, no. She said her daughter didn't confide in her, so she couldn't give us a name to work on. And I'm afraid I got nothing out of her about yesterday morning. Apparently, she takes sleeping pills and wears earplugs too.'

'That's what her daughter told me. She's very distressed, of course, and not in good health either . . . odd that they weren't at all close . . . they look alike.'

As plump as a pigeon with six holes puncturing her smooth belly, four of them hitting almost the same spot . . . the opening . . . washed before these photographs . . .

'Pretty . . . I expect the sister's like her father, being dark-haired and so on.'

'Yes. Yes, he is dark—not so slim, though. Put a lot of weight on with the years—haven't we all? He'll have to be more careful now, I would imagine. Tidy shot. Short range, of course, apart from the last shot; no burn marks, though. I'm pushing for the autopsy report for tomorrow morning but I've already had a word with Forli. Technically, cause of death was the bullet in the back of the head, instantaneous, very little bleeding. She would have died anyway from the other wounds.'

'Yes. The missing bullet . . .'

'I've told them I want it found today. I've looked at the video of the area near the body and it looks from the enhancement as if the most likely thing is it went through the photograph that was smashed. It's got to be lodged there somewhere. I'm holding a press conference at six. Have to give them something. It's August and they're desperate. You needn't bother coming back. You have enough on your plate, and Maestrangelo will be here.'

Thank goodness for that. The captain was good at that sort of thing.

'Right, Marshal. I'll get a copy of the autopsy report to you as soon as I have it. Call me, of course if there are developments . . .'

'Yes . . . the sister was wanting to move the child back into his own room along with a maid. I explained—'

'No, no, no. The crime scene stays sealed. I'll speak to her. And, Marshal, I want to be kept informed of any and every development in this case. You've got my mobile number. Call me any time.'

'Of course.' Important people. But there were less-important people in this story, too.

'Is there something else?'

The marshal remained seated, hands firmly planted on his knees, his hat clutched between big fingers.

'Yes. Yes, the workmen. I promised to let them know whether they could carry on tomorrow. They'd be working on the disused outbuildings, mostly on the roofs. The area's been searched.'

'Yes, well, that shouldn't be a problem.'

Some people could go to bed happy then. The marshal wasn't among them. Well, he wasn't going to eat alone in the kitchen. It was too depressing. After a battle with That Thing over the daily orders for tomorrow, he showered and changed and went to the NCO's club to eat supper. He ate with a recently retired man who had taken a job with an industrialist.

'All he really wants is for me to be there so that when he has to be away I act as his eyes. I really don't have to do much, and it's decent pay.'

'You don't get bored?'

'Now and again, but there are plenty of people to chat to.'

With a good meal under his belt, he escaped from one of those depressing 'Did you hear So-and-so died' conversations and the prostate problems of long-retired colleagues and got home just in time to catch the tail end of what the late edition of the regional news was saying about his case. He turned off the television and wandered through the rooms as though he were looking for

43

something. The rooms were empty and silent, and what he wanted he wasn't going to find there. Far too late to call her now. He could have called her before he went out to the club and he had to confess to himself, now, that he hadn't done it because she'd have asked him again about the flat he hadn't done anything about. Well, tomorrow he would be seeing the captain. He'd talk to him about it then and call Teresa tomorrow evening. He went to bed and fell into a dreamless sleep, only to open his eyes suddenly at five in the morning, wide awake and with two questions in his head. The man was cold-blooded, watching her crawl away from him all that time, but why did the prosecutor think the man was such a tidy shot when there was a missing bullet, meaning he'd missed a dying target since he could hardly have missed her when she was facing him in the doorway? And why did that woman wear earplugs in a place as silent as a graveyard?

'The bulldozer,' he answered himself aloud, shutting his eyes again. That was it. She liked to sleep late. 'And until they find the bullet . . . that's Forensics' problem.' He turned over, pummelled Teresa's pillow, pulling it to himself, and went back to sleep.

Three

The morning was stale and dank. If only it would really rain. Sometimes you felt a few tiny drops, but it never amounted to anything except an increase in the general humidity. The buildings in the city looked dirty, and with fewer cars you could smell more drains. The marshal's driver was nosing his way out into Piazza Pitti, pushing through trailing groups of tourists instead of traffic. The marshal had retreated behind his dark glasses from the colourless glare. After a brief visit to the the Faculty of Science out on Viale Morgagni and an hour's desk work, he already felt he wanted to take another shower.

They crossed the Ponte Santa Trinita. The river was low and sluggish. People were taking photographs of each other with the Ponte Vecchio in the background. All the colours were drab and the hills upriver were invisible.

'Will you want me to wait for you, or should I come back later?'

'Wait for me. You can drive me up to the villa afterwards.'

But when they reached Headquarters in Via Borgo Ognissanti, the marshal saw the captain sitting in his car as it was drawing out of the cloister. The driver stopped the car and the window went down on the passenger side.

'I'm sorry, Guarnaccia. It's an emergency. There's been another episode at the gypsy camp and the press are all over it, attacking the mayor for giving them a permanent camp, and so on. He needs an update and some advice before he calls a press conference at the Palazzo Vecchio. Come with me and get me up to date on your business. Your driver can follow us.'

The marshal instructed his driver and got into the captain's car.

'How's it going?'

The marshal thought a moment and then said, 'Oh . . . I don't know. It's . . . difficult. Nothing you can get a handle on, nobody with anything to say. The wealthy middle classes . . . you just can't tell what's really going on . . .'

'And you're afraid things are not as they seem?'

'Well, they hardly ever are, are they? But, I mean, none of it makes much sense to me—for a start, why buy a place like that just to pull it apart and change it into something else? What's the point?'

'I agree with you. I saw the place, years ago, when it was abandoned. There were a lot of those medieval villas once—you can still see them in paintings, but most of them disappeared long ago—within a two-mile radius of the city, more or less. And they were the wealthy middle classes of their day, you know, the people who built them.'

'Oh . . . I thought they'd be the big names, the nobility.'

'Not at all. The important families operated from their country estates, much further out. No, these were merchants, bankers and so on. It was good insurance, growing a bit of food and wine, having somewhere to hide from enemies and plagues.'

'I suppose it was. He's wrecking the place, anyway, in my opinion—not that I'm setting myself up as a judge of architecture.'

'I'm sure you're right, but it happens all the time that these rambling places get divided up. As often as not, the banks buy them. Speculation.'

'But he lives there.'

'So perhaps he'll sell up once all the work's done. Probably make a fortune.'

'Mmph.'

'All right. You're not to be moved. Did you get anything useful from the university?'

'Nothing, except that she was an exceptionally good scholar. She was hoping to stay on as a researcher, which is of no interest to us except . . .'

'Except?'

'The professor who was supervising her thesis—I managed to have a word with him, and that was a piece of luck because he stays at his house on the coast for most of August and he'd only come back to pick up some stuff for a paper he's working on.'

'And? What about him?'

'Nothing. They just seem to have been close. I get the impression she was ambitious. After all, apart from the child, she seemed to have no life at all beyond her studies. I just thought . . . ambitious young ladies sometimes, you know . . . shortcuts . . .'

'I thought that only happened in the entertainment industry.'

'No . . .' The captain didn't get out much, any more than Daniela Paoletti had. 'It happens in all fields. In fact, the professor himself told me that competition in the academic world is ferocious and that people with the right connections tend to win out over the really brilliant.'

'And would he have been the right connection for her?'

47

The marshal shook his head. 'They were only intending to take on one researcher next year, and there was the son of a politician in line for it—besides, the professor didn't look like he'd be up to it . . .'

'Really? What do you mean? Too old?'

'That, too. Never looked up from his books, I'd say. I can't see him making a nuisance of himself with young female students. I can't see him making a nuisance of himself with his wife—well, you shouldn't judge. After all, the victim sounds to have been the same type—and she did have a child. But no, it was a dead end. He had an alibi anyway: He was in Naples for two days when it happened, working on something I didn't understand with two other academics. You can tell what sort he was by the fact that it didn't cross his mind that it was an alibi I was after, and he started telling me about this paper on whatever it was. I'd still be there now if somebody hadn't interrupted us and saved me. Reminded me of Professor Forli. No, no . . . dead end . . .

'I talked to two women and a man in the registrar's office, but they didn't see that much of her. They were amazed when I told them how she died, but they didn't have a scrap of information about any boyfriend. Not even hearsay, gossip, nothing. And as for the child's father, they didn't even know she had a child. I left my card. They obviously wanted to see the back of me this morning. They had an endless queue of foreign students to enrol.'

'Someone must know, for heaven's sake. Florence is supposed to be a hotbed of gossip. What's the prosecutor saying?'

'He's saying Find the boyfriend. What else can he say? Good heavens, I see what you mean about the press. Television, as well.'

They were driving across the Piazza della Signoria to the municipal offices in the Palazzo Vecchio. Huge groups of sweating tourists were following flags or umbrellas held aloft.

'What happened at the gypsy encampment? I missed most of the news last night.'

'A man was stabbed in the leg yesterday by a group of gypsy children in a bag-snatching episode near the station and then, during last night, somebody managed to get into the camp and set fire to two house trailers with a can of petrol. A little girl died.' They got out of the car and, on the instant, a telecamera was there.

'Channel three news. Can you tell us anything . . . ?'

The captain ignored them. 'I'm not likely to be in the office much, Guarnaccia, but you can get me on my mobile—and that press conference may well be put off until tomorrow because we'll have to hold one about this business, as you can see.'

'I imagine so. Funny . . . I'd been thinking that the murder of a well-to-do victim would get all the attention, but it's a little gypsy girl.'

'It's not the little gypsy girl the mayor's worrying about, it's his political future. Keep me informed.'

'I will.' As the marshal got back into his own car, he remembered about the flat for sale. Too late. The driver started the engine. The cameraman was pushing through the tourists to hurry into the building behind the captain. A couple of youngsters in shorts and baseball caps stopped licking their ice cream and turned to stare after them. That cameraman was wasting his time. The journalists' nickname for Captain Maestrangelo was 'The Tomb'.

*　　　　*　　　　*

'We should have found it before, of course.' The technician exhibited the bullet in a small plastic bag.

It was hardly surprising. The bedside cabinet was antique, deeply carved, and damaged by ancient woodworm scars.

'It had literally disappeared into the woodwork! If we hadn't known it had to be here, we'd have been hard put . . .'

'The prosecutor will be pleased.' Not that the marshal himself wasn't, it was just that he wanted to be alone in the room and he hadn't yet had the chance, apart from a very few moments yesterday. Too many people all over everything.

If the people in this family told him nothing, then perhaps the house itself would tell him things.

The windows were closed and shuttered and the lights on. It seemed gloomy for a few moments after the forensic people had taken their powerful lights away, but he waited and the effect soon passed.

Plastic sheeting had been put over the bed and the floor beside it so that the sister could be brought in here yesterday. The marshal removed these now and put them out in the corridor.

Then he stood still for a long time, looking.

The tumbled, snowy bed, red floor tiles, smooth with centuries of wax and wear, the few pieces of furniture, dark and heavy. It might be a convent cell . . . except for that one area of disorder, the

50

messy trail leading to a chalk outline. Broken glass from the photo frame. The picture, with its frame and backing, had been laid flat on the bedside table to be photographed by the technicians. A little blond girl in white, a First Communion picture with a small round hole in it. The marshal looked at the child Daniela. She'd been very thin then, and her big solemn eyes were ringed with dark shadows. Nobody in this family seemed to be in the best of health, one way or another. There were two other photographs by the bedside lamp, one of Daniela holding her baby in his christening robe, the other a more recent one of little Piero pushing a wooden truck with red wheels. Yesterday's search had turned up no other photographs. On the floor above, in Daniela's big tidy study, the marshal had found a desk diary which contained nothing personal at all. There was the odd dental appointment, tutorials for her thesis, reminders about picking up dry-cleaning. If the man was married, then he had certainly been able to count on her discretion. It looked as if she would succeed in taking her secret to the grave. At the very top of the tower was an attic. It was empty.

'She never really talked to us.'

An attic without secrets, a diary without secrets.

She had a secret, though.

The child's bedroom was small and cheerful, the bedclothes turned back to air, a fur animal of some sort with a pointed nose propped on the pillow. A shelf of picture books. The bathroom was tidy, mostly white. Towels, some white, some dark blue, were folded on the brass rail, all except a used one lying on a linen basket.

A quiet, studious woman had got up, washed and dressed her little boy, given him his breakfast on the floor below, and taken him down to her sister. Had she then come up and taken a shower? Possibly. She'd still been wearing some sort of white robe when she died, and she hadn't had time to make her bed. This was no place for a murder. It was all so quiet, so clean and simple, so . . . innocent.

Nothing is what it seems. Even the house phone . . .

He looked again at the chalk outline of her body.

Perhaps she tried to raise herself to reach the telephone but sank down just as he fired at her head the first time.

And still, what help was it to know that? Somebody had come up here and she had opened the door to her killer. Had she known him? She must have. She had opened the door to him in her robe, a thin, white robe, silk, maybe. There was no house phone up here, and he hadn't seen one on any floor yesterday. He walked to the window above the entrance and opened it up. Hard to recognize anyone from directly above at this height, but somebody familiar, a voice calling up a greeting . . . He leaned out.

There was a man standing down there.

His hair was dark. He wasn't in uniform. He was smoking. Suddenly, he looked left and right, tossed the cigarette, and ducked under the police tape to get in.

The marshal closed the window and started down. There was little point in trying to do it silently on the stone stairs. How the devil this man had got in was a mystery since the grounds were still full of carabinieri, but the marshal was more interested in who than how. When he reached the ground floor the man was there, looking around.

'For God's sake!'

'Morning, Guarnaccia.'

'What the devil are you doing here—and how did you get in?'

'Oh, you know me,' Nesti grinned.

'Yes, I do, and it's lucky for you the prosecutor's not here or he'd put you away for this. Get out.'

'Come on, Guarnaccia, give me something, anything, for tomorrow's paper and I'll go. Besides, I knew the proc wasn't here and I got in down near that cottage where they were searching until ten minutes or so ago. Wall's a bit broken down there—I've ruined my shoes.'

Nesti's obsession with being first on crime scenes was only equalled by his passion for fine clothes and shoes.

'Get out, Nesti.'

'I've helped you out before now.'

That was true. Nesti had been a crime reporter on *The Nazione* for longer than the marshal had been in Florence, and he knew just about everything there was to know about the place.

'Besides, I can't get out the way I got in, because the wall's two metres higher from the ground on the inside—and I can hardly go out the front gates. There's one of your cars parked there.'

'Nesti!'

'You'll be sorry if you don't help me out, because I've got something on this rogue.'

'On whoever killed her?'

'Maybe—though, if I'm right, you haven't a hope of catching him. No, I meant the owner of this

53

place, Paoletti. You won't have met him, he's in hospital.'

'And you have? Don't tell me you've been to the hospital—'

'No, no, no. A story from years back. He's gone up in the world, judging by the size of this place.'

'Nesti . . .' It was true that he was often useful, but he had this casual way of throwing out information so that you were never sure if he was serious—or, to be exact, you were always sure he couldn't be serious, but he usually was. There was something about his laconic delivery and the fact that his eyes were always squeezed almost shut—probably against his own cigarette smoke—that made everything he said seem comic.

'So: I leave here with you in your car, having been sent for by you to give you some background information on Paoletti. And you ought to give those two on the gates a bollocking for not noticing me coming in, to make it more convincing. That's the first problem solved.'

'And what's the next problem?'

'I told you: something for the crime page for tomorrow. I give you the goods on Paoletti and you give it back to me and I write it up. Everybody's happy. Only, if you don't mind, we'll do that over lunch because I'm starving and I haven't a bean.'

'You shouldn't spend it all on clothes.'

'You're right. And now I'm going to have to buy another pair of these shoes. We'll eat at Paszkowski. I need cigarettes and, besides, everything else decent is closed in August.'

'You've given up giving up smoking, then?'

'Not at all. I never give up giving up. Just giving it

54

a rest for a bit.'

'Well, we're not going anywhere for lunch—I haven't time to stop for lunch.'

Not for more than a couple of sandwiches, anyway. But in the end he agreed to have supper with Nesti. He might really have something useful to say, but the truth was that the marshal would have supped with the devil himself to avoid eating alone at home.

It had been like that when he was a lad. They never went on holiday, but his school friends did, and he'd hang around the house, not knowing what to do, morose and lonely. His mother was too busy to have any patience with him.

'Don't stand in the middle of the kitchen, I've the floor to mop. Go and play with Nunziata or else help your father with the hens.'

But his sister was two years older and didn't want him around. His father was quiet and patient, but it was easy to see that he got on better on his own.

Before long, he'd be back in the kitchen.

'I'm hungry.'

'Here. Have a slice of bread.'

She'd cut a thick crust and put a slice from a big tomato on it with salt and a drop of oil.

'Here. Now, get out from under my feet. Why don't you go and call for little Beppe. He'll play with you.'

'He's only eight!'

But he would go, in the end, and an instant friendship would be improvised and last through the long, lonely month of August until everybody was back.

He dropped Nesti further down the road where his car was parked.

'Eight o'clock at Paszkowski, then. In the

meantime, I think I'll go and take the waters. Good for my liver.'

'What . . . ?'

* * *

At five in the afternoon, the marshal was in his office. He'd looked in on the two lads in the duty room, one of whom was at the console talking to the motorbike patrol.

'Everything all right?'

'All quiet, Marshal.'

'All right. Look up this name, will you? See if there's anything on our records.'

'Right . . . isn't this the name—'

'Yes. Bring me anything you find right away—and if there are any reports of incidents involving gypsies, tell me. The captain wants to avoid whipping up hysteria—especially in the press.'

'Right. You know another child died?'

'No. What happened?'

'It's just come through. The little brother of the girl who died in the fire. He was badly burned. Died about an hour ago, poor kid. Let's hope that'll shame the anti-gypsy campaigners into shutting up.'

The marshal doubted it. Two gypsies less would be their only thought. He sat down behind his desk and sighed. It was an intractable problem around which emotions ran high, interest in facts low. Each time a small incident occurred, trouble would flare up—literally this time—and now it was a political football.

As a child, he had never really believed his parents' warnings about the gypsies, even though

56

they made him shiver under the bedclothes on windy nights. Why should they steal children? It was just one of those fairy stories they tell to keep you frightened into not wandering off or staying out in the dark. But gypsies do steal children, though not usually in Italy, and teach them to beg and steal. And even to stab people in the leg if they don't cough up, apparently . . .

He took out his notebook and opened it. Talk about intractable problems.

Costanza Donati, a good sort of woman you'd be glad to have as a neighbour, hadn't been able to help much as far as Daniela Paoletti's death, or even life, was concerned. She had been more than helpful, though, on another problem. Her husband was a doctor, a consultant, and she had promised to talk to him about getting Nunziata's therapy done in Florence if she needed it.

'It's not his field but, don't worry, he'll make the arrangements as soon as you give the word.'

'I'd really appreciate it. I've heard it makes people ill. She shouldn't be alone when she can be here with us. You're very kind.'

'Not at all. It's nothing compared to what you did for us.'

'How's your son doing now?'

They had talked for a while, sitting on a bench in the shade. The Donatis' garden was set high up, a good four metres higher than the road. There was a pretty good view of the top two floors of the tower from here.

'Too far to hear anything, though, I imagine.'

'I couldn't say. I might have heard something if that wretched bulldozer hadn't been going. I can't see what they're up to over there, but I'm willing to bet they're

57

wrecking that beautiful old place.'

A very good sort of woman.

'I must say, though, Marshal, to be honest, I don't know if I'd have noticed or recognized gunshots, anyway. I've only ever heard them on television or at the cinema. I enjoy a good crime story, if it's not too violent. Would it have been very loud?'

'No. Not like on television at all. Still, it's not really the time of the shooting that's a problem, it's whether you saw anybody, and you've already said not. Had you been out here some time, by the way? Perhaps the carabiniere who came over yesterday asked you that?'

'Yes, he did, and I told him I was out here by nine-ish. It's a long job, that and the dead-heading. It's my husband's job, really. He's the gardener. It's just that there was a bit of an emergency that morning and he left much earlier than usual. I saw the young woman's car going back in, and then she came running out screaming.'

She had gone inside and then come out through the French windows with a tray. Something cool to drink. The sound of pouring liquid, the clink of ice cubes, birdsong, and the smell of grass. It must be nice to have a garden. Lot of work, though.

'How is the family taking it, Marshal? It must have been such a shock. I can't say I see much of them, but they all go off to church together on Sunday mornings—I rarely go myself, I must confess, and my husband's a regular Florentine priest-hater. She was so young . . . the little boy always sits on her knee in the car. That's really the only time I see them. Elio and I have breakfast out here in good weather. How's the sister coping? My goodness, she was in a state.'

'She's calmer today.'

'Even so, it's a worry. That little boy will need her . . .'

'Yes. I just wish I knew who the father was.'

'That I don't know. And I've never seen her with a man. I'm sorry.'

The marshal was sorry too. He closed his notebook now and sat staring at the map of his quarter on the opposite wall. There was precious little to add to his case notes from that interview, other than that they all went to church together. Not entirely a waste of time, though, if her husband would help out with Nunziata. The family should all be together, especially in times of trouble. He'd telephoned Teresa right away to tell her.

'But what if she doesn't want to? We all like to be in our own homes. You, of all people, should understand that.'

'But not alone. And not when we're ill. She's bound to feel upset and to need looking after.'

'She's perfectly calm and organized. She's here now and she's shaking her head.'

'Let me talk to her.'

And Nunziata had taken the receiver and laughed at him.

'That's you all over. The Tyrant of Syracuse!'

'What?'

'Don't you remember?'

'Remember what?'

'Dionigi! The Tyrant of Syracuse! That story they told us at school—what was that teacher's name? I forget—anyway, the one who used the throw the chalk at you because you could never remember your subjunctives. Surely you remember the story—the old woman who prayed for Dionigi when he was dying,

59

when everybody else wanted to see the back of him!'

'I don't—you're not dying—'

'And when they asked her why, she said she wanted him to stay alive because whoever came after him was likely to be worse—and she was right, too!' Roars of laughter. *'I called you the Tyrant of Syracuse for months afterwards! Don't pretend you've forgotten. From the minute you were half an inch taller than me, you always had to be the boss.'*

'Mmph.'

'Well, you're still bigger than me, but you can play the tyrant all you like. I'm not going anywhere. I've got everything organized here, and I've no intention of dragging my carcass to somebody else's house to be ill. Teresa's got her work cut out as it is, with you and the children. Now get off the line. We have to go out. 'Bye, Tyrant of Syracuse!'

'Well, it's not right,' declared the marshal to the map on the wall. He remembered once having a really bad bout of flu years ago when he was here by himself, tormented by fever, embroiled in nightmares, unable to keep anything down except water and sometimes not even that. His head spinning each time he had to get up and drag the sweat-soaked sheets off yet again.

'No, no . . .'

A carabiniere tapped and put his head round the door. 'Did you call?'

'What? No.'

'Oh. I thought . . . I was just going to tell you: There's nothing on Paoletti. No criminal record.'

'All right.'

The carabiniere retreated, and the marshal remembered that he hadn't called the bank about that mortgage. Just as well Teresa hadn't asked

60

him. Tomorrow. But tomorrow was Saturday and the bank would be closed. Damn! He decided to do the daily orders and switched on That Thing. Something to focus his ill humour on.

* * *

Piazza della Repubblica had a dark, deserted air despite a couple of bars and a restaurant that remained open for tourists. The colonnade running in front of the central post office was empty of its usual newspaper kiosks, and almost all the shops had their metal shutters down. Paszkowski's outside tables were surrounded by potted hedges hung with fairy lights, which should have been cheerful but somehow looked a bit sad. A band was playing wearily.

'Christ, this clammy weather,' was Nesti's greeting. 'Unless you want to sit sweating out here, let's get inside to the air-conditioning.'

A waiter in cream jacket and dark gold tie passed them, holding high a tray full of huge, brightly coloured drinks with flags and fruit bobbing about on sticks.

One of the barmen greeted Nesti.

'A quiet table. We need to talk.'

'Mario! A table.'

They were led to a quiet area where only one couple sat eating. The man had a gigantic, elegant white dog on a leash. It raised its long head and showed a set of perfectly white teeth and a lolling pink tongue, then slumped down again.

'What can I bring you?'

'Two of your aperitifs and a menu—and, Mario, a pack of cigarettes.'

They both ordered pasta and when he'd tasted his, the marshal said, 'It's really good . . .'

'It's always good. You sound surprised. Don't tell me you've never eaten here.'

'Of course not; why would I?'

Nesti shrugged. He had put his fork down to light up. 'There's nowhere else to go when it's late at night and you need something decent to eat and you've run out of fags.'

'Do they allow smoking in here?'

'No. Listen: this Paoletti chap.'

'I've run a check. He has no record.'

'Maybe not, but he has a history.'

'Of what?'

'Pimping.'

'Pimping?'

Nesti stubbed out his half-smoked cigarette and took up his fork again. His face was perfectly serious. 'Down the Cascine Park. He was arrested for beating a prostitute to within an inch of her life. Can't find out why. Probably trying to cheat him—or, even more likely, trying to get away from him. She was very young.'

'But there was obviously no conviction.'

'No. That's why it's interesting. She was found by punters driving through the park, lying in the road covered in blood, and one of the other prostitutes named him as her pimp. But there was no proof, and the victim couldn't testify against him, so he got off.'

'You mean she died? Or was she just too scared?'

'Neither. She couldn't testify against him because she was his wife. It took them a while to find him, and when they did he'd married her *and* convinced the priest who did the job that he was saving her

62

from the streets. Saved himself from a good stretch, more like—pimping, grievous bodily harm. The minute she came out of hospital, he snatched her up and by the time they arrested him, he'd married her. If she hadn't been a prostitute, she might have been given some protection as a witness, but . . . and the priest made a statement as a character witness. I'll send you a copy of the articles about it tomorrow, if you like.'

'Thanks. Where did she end up, I wonder . . .'

'I can tell you that. Drop more wine?'

'Yes . . . thanks. That's a very fine wine you ordered.'

'You don't want to be drinking cheap wine, it's bad for your liver. I'm sorry I'm broke, but it'll be my treat next time. Anyway, so she ended up a princess in a fairytale castle, where you found her. What did you think of her?'

The marshal was stunned, so much so that, at first, he connected the young prostitute found bleeding in the park with the murdered young woman found in the tower. But, of course, it was the mother, the frightened, silent, glassy-eyed mother. And what made Nesti's story inescapably credible was the bit about the priest.

They all go off to church together on Sunday mornings.

Four

By the time they left Paszkowski's, they'd done themselves pretty well, between them, and the walk back across the river was much needed. They took the Ponte Vecchio which, though it was dark with all the shops battened down under their wooden shutters, was at least a little bit busier than the other bridges with perfumed after-dinner holidaymakers and couples kissing on the balustrade in the middle. Once they were on the other side, silence fell and they could hear nothing but their own footsteps in the sweltering night.

'Just as well I went to take the waters today,' said Nesti, giving his paunch a friendly pat. 'Should stand me in good stead digesting all that.'

'You weren't serious?'

'Well, no. I didn't actually drink any of the foul stuff, if that's what you mean. But I went there.'

The marshal looked sideways at him, but there wasn't enough light to make out his expression. As always, a cigarette dangled from his mouth, its end glowing, his eyes screwed almost shut against the smoke.

'God, those watering places are dire. Of course, they don't do as much business as they did in the days when it was so easy to book in for your wining and dining, gambling and nightclubbing on the National Health—though you lot can still get away with it on your insurance, can't you? You ever try it?'

'No.'

'No liver problems?'

'Now and again, but my wife would never leave the children and you won't catch me in a hotel alone.'

'You wouldn't be alone long, if my little visit was anything to go by. I told you Paoletti had gone up in the world. Got a very fancy nightclub now, catering to the rich and particular who don't mind leaving their wives at home so as to indulge their specialized tastes while taking the waters.'

The big stones of the Palazzo Pitti glowed yellow in the lamplight, and they paused at the bottom of the forecourt to finish their conversation, their voices lowered in the silence of the night.

'The Emperor, it's called. I told you I could help you.'

'Well, it tells me where his money's coming from. I can't say the daughter's story about a staffing agency explained it.'

'It does, though, officially. It's his cover. Perfectly legal operation—only there's more staff coming into the country than you'll find on the files in that office, if you follow me, and we're not talking cooks and cleaners.'

'Prostitutes?'

'From Eastern Europe. Leopard never changes his spots. The staffing agency's useful because he can give a few girls real jobs and word gets around that it's legit. And I think there's more to it than that. I'll be going back there. I reckon there's a story in it, and a big one.'

'And will it produce a murderer?'

'More than one. If somebody's out to punish Paoletti—and attacking the family is just their style—it's because he's overstepping the mark. Importing prostitutes from ex-commie countries for his own place is one thing, but supplying other clubs, if that's what he's doing, that's Russian mafia territory.'

'Well, if that's the case, I can sleep easy. Nobody will expect me to deal with that.'

'True. Might get me the front page, though.'

They were about to part company when they heard running footsteps in the dark and a woman's voice screaming.

'Bit of business for you, Guarnaccia . . .'

The woman came into view, still running, as she passed under a lantern on the other side of the road. It was impossible to make out what she was screaming: Her voice was too high-pitched and hysterical. She was escaping from a big man who was running after her in silence.

The marshal was about to cross the road. Behind him, Nesti remarked, laconic as ever, 'I wouldn't like to be in his shoes if she turns on him.'

The marshal stopped. 'You know them?'

'Seen them around. They're rubbish. Drugs, small-time theft, pathetic.'

'Even so . . .' The marshal was inclined to agree that the overweight silent man pursuing her might well be in danger from the woman's fury. Her rage seemed to make the air vibrate.

'Get away from me! Fucking bastard! Get away from me!'

He had caught her and blocked her in the doorway of a bank.

'Leave them to it,' advised Nesti.

'Come across with me. If he sees us watching, he'll not hit her.'

They went and stood close.

'Come on, now,' the marshal said quietly, 'let her

66

be. Let her calm down.'

The big man ignored him. He clutched her arms.

'Let me go! Get away from me!' Her face looked a yellowish white. She wasn't breathing properly. She tried to protest, but her eyes turned up and she was collapsing.

'Nesti, call an ambulance.'

She was down on the pavement, her whole body rattling in a fit. Her legs began to jackknife. The marshal knelt and tried to keep her mouth open.

'Is she epileptic?'

The big man was kneeling, too, but all he did was to keep hold of her arm in a vise-like grip. He didn't answer.

'Is she epileptic? Answer me!'

'She takes some pills . . . or else injections. Injections . . . maybe she's asthmatic . . .'

'Lift her feet up! Oh, for God's sake . . . Nesti, lift her feet up. Is the ambulance coming?'

'On its way. I think she's coming round a bit.'

'Let go of me.' But the man kept his grip on her arm. 'Let me go! I can't breathe! I can't breathe!'

'You can breathe,' the marshal said. 'You are breathing. You're talking, so you're breathing, aren't you? Just lie still. There's an ambulance coming.'

'No! No! I'm not going to hospital! I don't want to go to hospital! Let me go!'

But her voice was feebler now and she didn't move.

When the ambulance turned up, it took some time to calm her protests sufficiently to get her onto the stretcher, but the ambulance men were very patient and they at last managed to loosen the man's grasp on her as they lifted her inside. He tried to get in with her, but they blocked him. After some argument, the ambulance left and the piazza was silent again.

'Well, I'm off. Got an article to write. We'll be in touch.' Nesti lit a cigarette and disappeared into the night, his footsteps echoing down a nearby alley.

The big man was still standing there, his arms dangling.

'You'd better be going home,' the marshal said. 'She's in good hands.'

He didn't answer or even look at the marshal. His lower lip dangled. He only had one bottom tooth. He seemed to be in a complete daze. The marshal wondered if it was drugs, or alcohol.

As if in answer, a stream of wine-dark vomit spouted from the dangling mouth, splattering on the pavement and spraying up the marshal's beige trousers.

The man remained immobile, as if he hadn't noticed. The marshal crossed the road and climbed the wide emptiness of the forecourt to the Palazzo Pitti. At the top, he paused before going under the archway to the left and turned to look back. Below, in the gloom, he could just make out the man's form, still standing in the bank doorway.

How do you get red wine stains off beige cloth? The marshal had no idea. He had something else on his mind anyway. He didn't go and change right away, but unlocked his station and looked in at the empty waiting room. Facing him were the two cells, their cream-painted doors bolted. A long time since they'd had to use one.

'Yes . . . that's it . . .'

Years ago, that man, Forbes. Nasty bit of work he

68

was, and he'd vomited litres of red in his cell the night they picked him up. And that was it: the unpleasant memory brought up by the faintest trace of a smell. Alcohol and vomit, cleaned up but still in the air. In that big fancy kitchen in the cellar, it was almost imperceptible but it was there. That's why the mother was too dazed to react to her daughter's death. The sweating, the glazed eyes . . . an almighty hangover. And, given what Nesti had told him, it was hardly surprising.

*　　*　　*

The afternoon heat was oppressive. Without the builders, not even the cement mixer broke the silence. The marshal reached the shelter of the cool stone portico and rang the bell. A young woman opened up. Blond, almost colourless hair tied back, jeans, a cheap-looking T-shirt. He followed her down to the kitchen. To understand this family, you had to fit into its timetable. At this hour, both the girls who did the household chores should be there—and the marshal was willing to bet that it was only their day job—and the lady of the house would be out of bed, cleaned up, and in a fit state to talk to him should she want to.

He was more or less right. She was sitting at the big glass table with a cup of something in front of her and a plate with the remains of some dry toast, but she wasn't dressed. She was in her nightdress with a wrap of some sort over it.

'I'm sorry to have to disturb you again . . .'

When he sat down, he got the yeasty warm smell of sleep and sweat coming off her, with a cloying hint of alcohol.

'Maybe . . . some coffee . . .' She looked from the marshal to the girl, uncertain.

'If you mean for me, no, Signora. I've only just had one on my way here.'

That was a lie, but he wouldn't have wanted to drink anything in here, not even a glass of water. He couldn't help it, he was keeping his breathing shallow again.

'I'll get on, then . . .' The girl hesitated and, when there was no answer, went through the door that was standing ajar, perhaps to her room. Would she be the one who had been watching him from the barred windows at his feet the other morning, or was it the other one?

'I understand from your daughter that you have someone staying here now, and I'm glad to hear it—would that be the young woman who's just left us? What's her name?'

'Danuta.'

'And she sleeps here now? Helps with the little boy?'

'I don't . . . perhaps, sometimes . . .'

It was obvious that she didn't know.

'Or perhaps the other young woman? The one I haven't seen?'

She didn't answer right away but lifted the cup to her lips very carefully, as though it were brimming over, but it wasn't. The problem was that her hands were trembling. Her forehead was beaded with sweat and her head must have been throbbing. Frowning with the effort, she said, 'It might be Frida. I'm sorry, I should be dressed at this hour.'

She looked frightened, and her glance shifted to the staircase. She wasn't apologising to the

70

marshal. It must be Paoletti she was afraid of, even in his absence.

'I'm sorry. I'm not well.'

'I understand. Your daughter, Silvana, explained—and of course, now, after such a shock. Two shocks. Your husband and then your daughter.'

Again she lifted the cup and sipped.

'It's milk,' she said, as though he'd asked, 'with just a drop of coffee. Coffee on its own upsets me.'

'Well, yes, it's heavy on the stomach if it's strong.'

Should he even have come here? Yes. He couldn't imagine the prosecutor getting anything out of her. Hadn't he already tried? She'd surely have taken something for her hangover, and the milk and toast might settle her stomach sufficiently to enable her to talk. Even though he was thinking this, he was taken aback when she put down the cup and said without expression, 'Is my daughter dead?'

'Yes, Signora, she's dead. In fact, I came here today to tell you that, now that the autopsy is done, the prosecutor will soon give his permission for you to bury her. You'll want to be making arrangements.'

'I can't do that. It will have to be when my husband comes home.'

'Yes, of course. I understand.'

'Where is Piero?'

'I'm not sure . . . I expect his aunt is looking after him.'

'By herself? Silvana musn't be left to look after him by herself.'

'No, you're right. She's still very upset—but now she has someone staying here who can help.'

71

'You have to excuse me. I'm ill.'

The marshal got to his feet and out of range. He knocked on the door, closed now, through which the girl had gone. 'I think the signora needs your help.'

The girl came out. She said nothing to him but went over to the woman. 'Do you want to get dressed now?'

'Bathroom. I feel sick . . .'

The marshal judged that she had forgotten his presence. The girl was helping her to her feet. In the doorway she had come through, he saw buckets and mops, and from there came that faint, now recognizable smell, masked by disinfectant.

'I'll see myself out.'

'Thanks.'

'Is there a time of day when the signora might feel up to talking, do you think?'

She shrugged her shoulders with a slight grimace that said more than her words. 'You could try just before supper, about sevenish. Signora! Don't hold on to the table. Lean on me—no, on me! That's better.'

The marshal climbed up to the fresh air out of doors and heard water splashing. He walked to the rear of the carriage drive and turned left towards the tower. In the blue pool, water running off her brown limbs and long hair, Silvana held a plump, blond cherub of a boy above her head. The cherub, with his curls all wet, was crying, but she laughed up at him until he stopped and laughed with her. The marshal stood a moment, watching, remembering Giovanni at that age, plump and brown, soft dark hair and huge brown eyes, amazed by the sea, not knowing whether to laugh or cry when the waves splashed over him. So little time they'd had before he'd had to leave. Even less with Totò. Nobody could give him back those years. A thin, fair girl was carrying a tray of sandwiches and drinks to the table under the umbrella. Must he barge in on this scene, a uniformed stranger come to talk about a funeral? It wasn't that urgent if nothing was to be done until Paoletti came home and he was going to have to come back, anyway, to try again with the mother. He retreated.

*   *   *

'Lorenzini! Thank God for that!'

Lorenzini was a bit taken aback.

'Well, it's nice to know I've been missed . . .'

Lorenzini, the marshal's second in command, was a dyed-in-the-wool Tuscan and had little patience with the marshal's Sicilian ways which, in his opinion, were convoluted, time-wasting, and, above all, irritating. They rarely agreed on anything, but they were used to disagreeing with each other and didn't take much notice of it.

'I saw the press conference about the gypsy children on the news. Maestrangelo looking as black as thunder, I suppose because of the political involvement.'

'Hmph.'

'You don't look too chirpy yourself. Teresa not back yet?'

'No.'

'I know how you feel. My wife's staying on for the rest of the month in Castiglioncello. Better for the kiddie, of course . . .'

73

'Oh, yes . . . '

'That's why I'm here now, instead of coming in tomorrow morning as I should. I thought we might have a bite together this evening.'

'Well, I was going to do my night round . . .'

'No problem. We'll have a bite and I'll come with you. Better than sitting at home watching those old films they put on in August—and I know just the place to go where we can cool off.'

Olmo is so high up above Florence that the temperature can be a good four degrees cooler. When they got out of the car, the marshal sighed with relief.

'That really does make a difference.'

'Stupendous view, as well.'

But, as they crossed the road from the carpark, a gigantic fork of lightning struck the hills on the far side of the Arno Valley, and the chains and clusters of tiny lights running across the night scene were temporarily effaced.

'Somebody's having a big storm,' Lorenzini remarked. 'Let's hope we get it in the city too. Clear the air. It's a long way off but better sit inside, just in case.'

They sat in front of a huge window where they watched the dramatic storm as they ate.

Remembering Teresa's constant advice of 'Just don't overdo it,' the marshal said, 'I won't have any pasta.'

'Good idea,' agreed Lorenzini. 'I'll order a plate of mixed crostini, give us something to chew on while we're waiting—I thought we'd share a Florentine beefsteak, what d'you think? With just a green salad and maybe a few chips . . .'

Perhaps the marshal really had been missing his

colleague. At any rate, he found nothing to disagree with there. Besides, eating was more of a pleasure in the cooler air. As the waiter poured him a glass of red, he almost sighed with satisfaction.

'So, what's this case the lads were telling me about? Anything interesting?'

'You could say that, I suppose, but it looks like it might turn out to be something a lot bigger than we thought, so it'll probably be taken off my hands. Can't say I'll be sorry, either. Did they tell you who the prosecutor was?'

'That was the first thing they told me.'

'Well, he's been all right—though, to be honest, I find it a bit hard to forget the way he behaved the first case I had to work with him—before your time . . .'

'No, it wasn't. That was my first year here, but you worked the case on your own.'

'Mmph. Well, I didn't want to get anybody in trouble . . .'

They demolished more than one prosecutor along with their beefsteak and then consoled themselves about being left alone in the heat of the city with a bit of pudding.

Gigantic fork lightning continued to attack the hills all around them.

'Spectacular! Did you see that?'

'What ? No . . .' The marshal was feeling for his wallet. This was a pretty fancy place . . .

'Sorry,' Lorenzini said. 'Just back. You know how it is. Must get some cash tomorrow. Shall we start the rounds?'

Their first stop on descending into dark waves of heat was outside the villa where two bored

75

carabinieri sat in darkness, their car parked just inside the gates, out of sight of the headlights of passing cars.

One of them got out and came to the gate to speak to the marshal.

'All quiet?'

'As the grave. Two young women left about nine. Nothing since.'

'Two? That's funny. I thought one was supposed to stay.'

The young carabiniere shrugged. 'There were two of them, dressed to kill, tits on them like—'

'In which car?'

'The mini.'

'Which way did they go?'

'That way, heading down to Porta Romana, I suppose.'

The marshal got back in the car. Either there'd been a change of plan and the second girl's services were required elsewhere, or she was driving the other one to the club and would come back.

They went down into the city. It was an uneventful round, the night air stale and close. The storm came no nearer. Around one fifteen, Lorenzini yawned.

'Shall we call it a day? God, I'm weary of this heat. I feel like I never went on holiday at all, I don't know about you.'

'Mmph. I'm grateful to have got through the day without anybody being sick on me.'

'What?'

'Nothing. Let's go. I'll tell you on the way.'

*　　　*　　　*

The marshal had been expecting to see Nesti's story in the next morning's *Nazione* but, going through it in his office as church bells rang all over the city, he found nothing. The crime pages were dedicated to the deaths of the two gypsy children, and there was a front-page article and an editorial too. Nesti would be disappointed, but he himself wasn't altogether sorry. His great friend the prosecutor would be very annoyed if the first he heard about Paoletti's goings-on was from the newspaper. Keep me informed of anything, he'd said, but what if there was nothing to it? Should he have used the mobile number late on a Saturday night? Paoletti had no record, there was nothing concrete, juridically speaking, and it was all so long ago. Still, just as well the paper hadn't run it. The other papers would be bound to start calling the Procura when it did come out. It would be no use looking for Nesti at this hour. He might be at his desk in the afternoon. He called the prosecutor and told him.

'I'll get on to Nesti later today and have him send you the articles that came out at the time. As I say, he wasn't convicted of anything, but he'll have spent a bit of time inside before being bailed and it seems he employed an ex-con as a gardener at one time, then sacked him. There could be a grudge . . .'

'Right. Good. Well done. We'll follow that up. I'll speak to Paoletti myself and get his name.'

'Yes. If you think I should go out to take a look round this club . . .'

'I should think a call to your people on the spot would be more useful. If there's anything going on, they'll know about it. I'll get on to them myself and have them call you.'

And he was as good as his word. Not a quarter of an hour had gone by and the church bells were still ringing when the marshal of the spa was on the phone. His name was Piazza and he was a jovial sort. Chatty.

'No, no, no! Journalists' gossip. The prosecutor called me and I popped in to take a look round, just in case, but there was nothing I didn't already know about. The place is above-board. Stag nights, business entertainment, private dinners and so on, you know the sort of thing. Very upmarket and very profitable. We're in the wrong job, if you ask me.'

'You're probably right.' He didn't bring up the question of the Russian mafia. You could never tell for sure whether Nesti was serious or not and, besides, he was a journalist, when all was said and done, and despite this being August, the paper hadn't run his story. 'Thanks for getting back to me quickly, anyway.'

'No trouble at all. Bad business about his daughter, though. Involved with some nasty character, I suppose. And him in the hospital, too. It happened here, you know.'

'No, I didn't know.'

'Oh, yes. He's not often here, but now and again when they're taking on new acts he comes to vet them. The manager was just saying to me, "He was right as rain, sitting at one of the tables with a coffee in front of him and we were listening to a singer for our stag nights." He said, "She was a redhead—decent-looking but useless, cracked up halfway through her song—when one of the lads

78

shouted 'Get your kit off and let's hope your tits are better than your voice!' I turned to him when she'd gone and said something. He just didn't answer. His eyes were open, he was sitting there normal as anything but he just didn't answer." He said, "I tried shaking him in the end but nothing. He couldn't hear me, wasn't compos mentis at all, so I called an ambulance." The manager said, "It makes you think," and I agreed with him. Still, they say Paoletti's going to be all right.'

'Yes, they're expecting him home soon.'

'Poor chap. Some homecoming that's going to be, with his daughter dead. Anyway, listen, you never know. After what you've told me, I'll be keeping a close eye on The Emperor. He may be above-board—and you can take my word on that— but he might have business competitors. You know what I mean.'

'Yes. That's what I was afraid of . . .'

'You're right to be. It wouldn't be the first time they've gone for an innocent family member. Anyway, don't you worry. You get on with following up your end of things and I'll have a chat with a few people here. If I hear anything at all, I'll be in touch.'

'Thanks. You know your people best.'

So why, then, did the marshal agree to go out to the club with Nesti that night? It was that decision, his and his alone, that was the cause of the trouble and he couldn't explain, at the time or afterwards, why he made it. Surely he couldn't have agreed to go out just to avoid being at home alone? No, no . . . although if Teresa had been here, she'd have advised him against it. But she wasn't here. She should have been here. With hindsight, of course, it was easy enough to put your finger on what didn't add up, but he didn't remember having registered anything then. And the only reason he'd called Nesti was to have those articles sent round to the Procura.

'No problem. I'll bring them myself. Have to go round there anyway. There's yet another press conference at six.'

'Gypsies?'

'What else? You going to be there?'

'No, no . . . Captain Maestrangelo will be dealing with that. I'm going back up to the Paoletti villa to see if I can get any sense out of his wife.'

'That should be interesting. Meet me afterwards at the newsagent's kiosk at Porta Romana. We'll go out and have a discreet sniff round at The Emperor. I've been hearing things.'

'What sort of things?'

'Tell you when we get there. We'll do everything on my credit card so your name doesn't need to come into it . . .'

Well, it was something, these days, if somebody else was going to pay . . .

'You can give me your half in cash,' he went on. 'Let's say half past eightish.'

*   *   *

When the girl opened the door to him, she looked terrified.

'It's Danuta, isn't it?'

She nodded, her eyes swivelling away from him to the kitchen staircase behind her and back to his uniform, balancing two kinds of fear. He smiled at her and stepped inside.

80

'What is it? Is Signor Paoletti home? It's all right. He'll talk to me—and I want to talk to you, too, afterwards.'

He wanted to reassure her, make her understand that he had other things on his mind than illegal immigrants, but that might be a bad idea, lose him the only advantage he had over Paoletti in the fear stakes.

'No. Let me go down first. You follow me.' He felt sorry for her and all he could offer was to place his solid bulk between her and her employer. As he walked down the stairs, he judged that he had interrupted a huge row. The air was still vibrating from angry shouts. Yet the only words he heard now were spoken very quietly.

'Get out.'

A chair scraped. The marshal went down the last steps.

'Good evening.'

His appearance was met with silence. The tension was palpable. Paoletti sat at the big glass table, which was laid for three. By his plate was a scattered pile of boxes of pills. Two of them had been ripped open. Paoletti's left hand lay on the table, his right covering it, holding it. His daughter stood with her back to a long marble worktop. Her hair was tied back with a white ribbon; her face was almost as white. A tap was running and the marshal could smell fennel.

'I see I've interrupted your preparations for supper. I'm sorry.'

'Not at all, not at all!' Paoletti recovered his wits at once. 'You must be . . . Marshal Guarnaccia, is that right? I've heard about you from the prosecutor. I'm very glad to see you. I know you're

81

doing your best to find out what happened to Daniela. Sit down, Marshal. Silvana, get on with what you're doing.'

She turned away and busied herself chopping the vegetables.

A chair had been pushed away from the table in front of one of the plates. Had he been shouting at his wife? The marshal, choosing a different chair, was certain that he had. He could smell, or at least sense in some way, her recent presence and her sick fear. Had she retreated to hide in the servants' quarters? There was nowhere else she could have gone when he told her to get out.

'Really, I came to talk to your wife. I didn't expect to find you . . .'

How could he finish that remark?

'You must be relieved to be home, in spite of everything.'

'Not in spite of but *because* of, as you put it, "everything." My daughter can't be left to cope alone. I discharged myself this afternoon. They want me back for some tests later, but I'm perfectly all right. Well? Is there any news?'

'Not yet, I'm afraid. We're still at the very beginning of our investigation—'

'I was told that the first forty-eight hours were crucial, that afterwards there's not much hope.'

'That's true sometimes. It's one of the reasons why I wanted to talk to your wife today.'

'She's not well enough. Besides, Silvana says she was asleep and knows nothing.'

'Yes. Still, as a matter of correct procedure.'

'Yes, yes. Well, another day. She's not in good health, and the shock of losing her daughter . . . If I can be of any help, even though I wasn't here . . .'

'There are one or two things I'd like to ask you, things of a personal nature about your daughter . . .' He could sense the girl, Danuta, still hesitating at the foot of the staircase behind him.

'Get upstairs.' Paoletti's face was heavy, but the skin of his cheeks was pasty and too loose, as though he'd lost some weight very quickly during his illness. His hair was white, and he had the same clear grey eyes as his daughter.

'Upstairs . . . ?'

'That's what I said!'

The marshal heard her scuttle back up the stone steps, confirming that the servants' quarters were occupied by his wife. He didn't order his daughter out of the room, so he wasn't going to say much.

'Well? What can I tell you?'

'It's about a gardener who once worked here.'

'Daddy, I didn't—'

'Get on! We'll be eating at ten o'clock, at this rate! Let me see, his name . . . Melis, Marco. I'm afraid I've no idea where he is now. You think he could be involved?'

'I thought he might have a grudge since you sacked him. For stealing, wasn't it?'

'I forget, to be honest. He was unsatisfactory, at any rate. I'll look back through my papers and see if I can at least turn up his last known address.'

'Thank you. The other thing is . . . as I'm sure you'll understand, your daughter's private life, the child's father, and so on. If you could . . .'

As he expected, the daughter was dismissed. 'Go upstairs.'

She went without a word. It seemed safe to assume that if his wife had disappeared into the servants' quarters rather than being sent upstairs like the others, it was so that he wouldn't see the condition she was in, that she was either drunk or still undressed or both. She hadn't been expecting her husband. Had he discharged himself when he heard that the marshal had seen her and was coming back this evening? The marshal waited to see what Paoletti would say next.

'Can I offer you something?' Playing for time.

'No. No, thank you.' It had to be a difficult performance. Wanting to be affable, cooperative, to deflect any interest in his business, but finding it difficult to combine that attitude with mourning for his daughter. Different expressions flitted across his face, to be instantly replaced by others. The marshal knew that he was trying on masks to look for a response. He was wasting his time. The marshal remained, solid, silent, and expressionless, immobile in his seat. He asked no questions, only watched Paoletti as he described his daughter's studiousness, her secretive nature, her silence over the pregnancy. The intonations, too, were tried on along with the masks. The marshal observed his rising tension, wondering if he would produce a tear when all else failed, remembering the priest who had been persuaded to be a character witness to a pimp all those years ago. He was running out of steam with no questions from Guarnaccia to help him; but this man had survived for years on the edge of the law and made a fortune. He was no fool.

'Now, you wanted to speak to my wife, and I'll arrange that for you the minute she's well enough. In the meantime, now you're here, you might as well have a word with Danuta, the girl who let you in. She wasn't here when it happened but—as you say—as a matter of correct procedure—routine inquiries, isn't that what you call it? Danuta!'

No doubt she'd been listening from the top of the staircase, and she started down at once.

'Bring me your papers, passport, work permit, everything!'

She scuttled back up and came back down with the papers. Her eyes never left Paoletti, and she was ready to jump to at his next order.

'Sit down there and answer the marshal's questions—her Italian's not wonderful, but she manages. I'll leave you to talk.'

He could afford to, knowing that, absent or present, he would be obeyed.

The papers were in perfect order, of course. As he looked at them, the marshal was listening to Paoletti's step on the stairs. Just a bit uneven.

'Tomaszów. Where's that? Near Warsaw?'

'No. Southeast, near the border with Ukraine.'

'Do you miss it?'

'It was cold.'

'So you're not one to complain about this August heat like we do.'

He asked no real questions, just kept her talking a bit about how many brothers and sisters, did she hope to go back one day, and so on. The purpose of Paoletti's move was to let him know that his operations were going to look perfectly legal on paper. Round one to him, but not entirely a waste of time for the marshal, who broke the rules by laying a big gentle hand on the frightened girl's head as he stood up to leave.

'Please don't worry. You're not in any trouble, and neither is Frida. Is she here?'

'She's putting Piero to bed.'

'Where?'

'Upstairs on the ground floor. They both sleep there.'

She wasn't pretty, too washed-out-looking. Her hair was so blond, it was almost white. It was tied back with a coloured elastic, the sort children wear.

He climbed the stairs. He had no thought of seeking out Frida. Her papers would be in order too, though Paoletti probably kept them locked up.

As he walked through the entrance hall upstairs, he heard voices and slowed down. A door stood open on his right to what looked like a pretty impressive library. He caught a glimpse of Silvana, turning, looking back over her shoulder, the hem of her full skirt between thumb and finger.

'For the office . . .'

'It's too short. You look ridiculous.'

She rushed out of the room and pushed past the marshal. She looked ready to burst into tears.

The marshal coughed. Paoletti appeared and closed the door behind him.

'Everything in order?'

'Yes. Don't let me keep you any longer from your meal.'

'I hope you'll forgive my wife—you can imagine what she's going through . . .'

'But of course! How could I not? Don't worry about it, nothing urgent. You need to concentrate on getting well. Your family needs you.'

Five

'Like they need a hole in the head,' was Nesti's comment. The marshal had found him waiting, standing in the dusk beside the shuttered newspaper kiosk, sleek as a cat in pale linens, cigarette parked in the corner of his mouth. 'I hope there's no chance of him turning up at the club tonight?'

'No, no. The marshal out there told me he very rarely goes there, and he's not recovered from his illness. I'd say he ought to be still in hospital, but he discharged himself.'

'Well, I hope you're right. God, I hate this city in August.'

There wasn't a single car on the big roundabout outside the Porta Romana, and the expanse of empty tarmac around a bulky white statue in the silent gloom felt odd, even a little sinister.

'The rest of the year, you can't breathe for the exhaust fumes; and now you can't breathe because there's no air. Like living in an armpit.'

'Why stay, then? You're senior enough at the paper to choose your holidays.'

'Got a bit of a story going and she has to stay, so . . . We'd better get moving. We said half past eight.'

'I had to go home and change. I could hardly go on this jaunt in uniform. I hope you know what you're doing.'

'Don't worry about it! We're two innocent punters looking for a bit of fun while the wives and kids are at the seaside!'

'Hmph. I haven't had time to eat, either, and it's your turn to pay.'

'This is business, not pleasure, though. We've got work to do.'

'A place like that won't open before eleven.'

'That's not what I mean. What I mean is, we've got a date. Are we going in your car or mine?'

'Both. I'd rather be independent. I'll follow you.'

The main street of the spa was as busy as Florence was quiet. It was completely dark by the time they got there and parked, and all the clubs, bars, and restaurants were lit, the more important clubs with flashing neon. Among the couples and groups in the street, a number of waif-like girls, obviously from Eastern Europe, wandered about, scanning the perfumed crowd.

'Looking for clients, I suppose,' commented the marshal.

'At this hour? No. Looking for some lone man to buy them a meal.'

They were certainly thin and must have needed feeding. That one there looked like Danuta. But then, they all did. It wasn't the features, it was the expression . . .

'Come on, Guarnaccia, you can't feed them all. We've already got a date, remember?'

Their date didn't look hungry. She was very pretty with long black curls, sparkly eyes and a great deal of self-confidence. She had worked The Emperor as a pole dancer for three months and left when her contract ran out. She was freelance, had an agent who found safe, well-paid gigs for her, and at the end of this season reckoned she'd have saved enough to go home to Rumania and go on with her university degree in economics. She almost had to shout to tell them all this, the restaurant was so crowded and noisy.

'And afterwards?' the marshal asked, offering her cheese for her pasta. 'Will you be able to find work there, or will you come back here?'

'Here? No. I've bought a few plots of land back home. Bought them for a pittance, but now we've joined the EU they'll be worth a fortune. I won't be coming back. Not that I've got anything to complain about. I've met some decent people.'

'Like my pal Tommaso,' suggested Nesti, putting down his fork and reaching for his cigarettes.

'It's no smoking here,' the marshal said, looking about him.

'Right,' agreed Nesti, lighting up, 'that's why there's an ashtray. You passed up a good chance there, you know, Maddalena.'

'Oh, Tommaso's all right. But he's got his job on the paper here. Sports reporting's his life. And then there's his family. His mother's widowed and she's not so well. He wanted me to stay here, get married. I've got my own plans. I intend to make money. A lot of money. Order me a grilled fillet steak, Nesti. It's the only thing fit to eat in this place.'

'You chose it.' Nesti snapped his fingers for a waiter without looking up.

'Because I've got to meet somebody in the bar next door at eleven, that's why.'

'Not above turning the occasional trick in the interests of getting rich, then.'

'Not if it's a decent sort and he pays well, no. It's an honest transaction. Look around you at the women in here with their lifted faces and Vuitton handbags—all paid for by hubby while they're

89

screwing his best friend. The difference between them and me is that their transactions are dishonest. Listen, I haven't a lot of time. Are you going on with this story or not?'

'I'm here, aren't I?'

'And what about him? Who is he exactly?' Her bright grey eyes transfixed the marshal.

'I . . .'

'He's all right. He's a friend of mine. Has some influence in the carabinieri, and it's going to be up to them in the end. I just want the front page. I'm not up for any dramatic rescue stuff.'

'Well, be careful. Do things her way, or there'll be no way anybody can rescue her.'

'Don't worry about that. What's her name?'

'Cristina, but don't ask for her by name. She'll be on the centre pole, and she'll be wearing a silver tanga and a transparent blue top that she'll take off while she's dancing. Her hair's pretty much like mine and she's got a mole, really dark, just under her left breast. When she comes offstage to work the room, she'll find you.'

'How many girls like her are there?'

'Five. But it's the other two, the ones you won't see, that really matter.'

* * *

The local marshal had certainly been right about one thing. The Emperor was upmarket, all right. Attended carpark, big, well-kept gardens all around, gravel paths discreetly lighted.

'This must cost a pretty penny in upkeep,' said the marshal. They could hear music in the distance.

'Bit more than the good old-fashioned brothels in the city, eh?'

'It was a mistake to ever close them.'

'Before you were old enough to get to try them, you mean? Or is that the cop in you talking? More control, medical checks, that stuff?'

'No, no . . . I just hate seeing those young girls out on the street at all hours, getting frozen and soaking wet, the poor little things. It's not right. They should be inside where it's warm.'

'Well, they're inside where it's warm here, all right.'

It might have been the foyer of a cinema with the box office to the left, a velvet curtain straight ahead, a staircase to the right.

'Two,' Nesti said.

'First-time customers?'

'Yes.'

'Thirty euros.'

'Visa all right?'

The marshal followed Nesti beyond the curtain towards the noise of disco music. They weren't going to be able to hear themselves think, let alone talk to this Cristina, whoever she was, in the marshal's opinion, but there was nothing for it but to go on with this line of inquiry, even if it turned out to be more use to Nesti's career than his own case.

The half-dark room lined with mirrors was about twenty-five to thirty metres long, with a bar at the far end and a stage halfway along on the left where three pole dancers were gyrating under spinning coloured lights. Small groups of leather sofas and armchairs were set around low tables. Nesti chose one they could have to themselves right opposite the stage. The place wasn't full but, then, perhaps it was early. Early for some. The marshal tried to smother a yawn.

'Something to drink?'

A waiter was leaning over them.

'No, no . . .'

'Don't want to look conspicuous,' Nesti said in his ear. 'It's included in the ticket price.'

'A glass of red then.'

Nesti relayed this and the waiter shook his head.

'They don't serve glasses of wine. Your ticket includes a real drink. Have a G and T like me. You can't not drink. We're here for a good time, remember?'

'A grappa, then.'

The waiter seemed satisfied with that and went away.

'I didn't know you liked grappa.'

'I don't, much!'

When it arrived, he sipped at it gingerly. 'And I don't like this noise!'

'What?'

'I don't—oh . . .' What was the use? He kept his face towards the pole dancers, trying to take in as much as he could of the customers without looking directly at them. Apart from three or four lone men of about his own age, they seemed to be all small groups of men in their late twenties, early thirties. He reconized the type. They usually had a job, still lived with their parents, and spent their salaries on cars, clothes, and holidays. Just the sort who could fritter away money in this place. It wasn't much money to fritter, though, was it? Fifteen euros, including a drink. Next drink would probably cost thirty, but even so . . .

The marshal started counting, still keeping his head towards the stage. He'd seen two men behind the bar, and as well as the waiter who'd served them, there was a waitress in a glittery bikini. Three pole dancers and more of the same working the room, stopping to kiss the lone customers, settling on the knees of the younger men. Must be at least three—yes, they were taking over the dancing now. That pair of dangerous-looking characters near the door were obviously bouncers . . .

He leaned towards Nesti's ear. 'They're not making any money out of this. There are more staff than customers in here.'

Nesti didn't answer, only nudged him. One of the dancers who had come off the stage was approaching them. Long dark curls and a mole under her left breast. Cristina. She sat on Nesti's knee and began kissing him and whispering in his ear. After a few minutes they got up and started towards the exit, and Nesti looked back to signal that the marshal should follow. As they came out, he murmured, 'It's worth a try.'

It wasn't. They were stopped at the cash desk.

'He must take another girl.'

'We both like this one. We'll pay for two.'

'No. That's sixty euros. Ten minutes.'

'Make that twenty minutes.' He pulled the girl close, grinning, and kissed her.

'A hundred and twenty.' He wound a plastic timer and gave it to the girl. They started up the stairs, and the marshal went back to the flashing darkness, the noise, and his grappa. This was going to be a long twenty minutes. He sat watching the pole dancers for a while, noting how their movements included eye contact and a seductive smile and how, every so often, tired out, their bodies would slacken and the smile melt away to be replaced by a glazed look of weariness. They never actually stopped moving, and the young men watching their breasts would never notice. They all had very pretty breasts. Some of them could really dance, too, while others just jiggled about and took up more or less obscene poses. Each time there was a changeover, a voice came over a loudspeaker exhorting applause for their brilliant performance. The response was feeble and would surely have been an embarrassment had it not been camouflaged by the pounding music. There had to be more than six girls, because someone had replaced Cristina. He looked at his watch and sighed inwardly.

'Can I take this?'

He nodded and Nesti's empty glass was picked up.

'Something else for you?'

'No, no . . .'

A blond girl with an electric blue bikini bottom and tattoos paused in front of him. He smiled at her and looked away. She moved on. They were very discreet. He thought about Maddalena, so bright and so determined to get her economics degree and make money. He couldn't help comparing her to the bored young men sitting around him. They talked and laughed and drank, and the naked girls were just accessories like the coloured lighting and the leather sofas. There was a stripper on the stage now, but the young men were still slumped in attitudes of boredom, even as she removed the last stitch and spread her legs to the mirrors reflecting her all around the room. Only three much younger boys sitting on the edge of the stage seemed awake and interested, but they, it seemed, were drunk and a bouncer warned them off when they tried to sit on the edge of the stage. They moved to the alcove just to the side of the stage, almost opposite the marshal. Two of them were giggling, but the other looked as though he wished he were at home in bed. Surely he couldn't be eighteen. He barely looked older than Totò. He sat leaning forward with his elbows on his knees, hands dangling, head down. Every now and then he gave a little jerk, like when you fall asleep in church. He didn't wake up even when, with a huge fanfare, a couple started miming a variety of sexual acts on the stage, the woman naked, the man half-dressed in black leather and wielding a whip.The two giggling boys fell silent and looked, but seemed puzzled. It was no wonder. They must have been hoping for excitement, and the whole fake performance was as sanitized and tidy and brightly lit as the meat counter at the supermarket.

What was more, twenty minutes must surely have gone by and Nesti, blast him, had still not come back. A young man wearing an orange baseball cap stopped to kiss one of the pole dancers in front of the marshal's table and yelled at a friend, 'Take a picture of me with your phone! Go on!'

Well, if the evening was boring, at least he'd be able to show off to his mates.

Surely that was Cristina . . . it was. She was slipping her top back on at the side of the stage.

'Round of applause for three talented girls! As talented as they're beautiful! Round of applause!'

Three girls left the stage and mixed with the customers as Cristina took her place at the centre pole and two others joined her on stage. There were nine of them then, by the marshal's reckoning. Cristina and her two, three who'd just come offstage and others around the room like the one being photographed with the boy in the baseball cap who must have had far too much to drink and whose antics were partly blocking the marshal's view.

'Another!' He leaned the girl over backwards, kissing her. 'Another!'

The camera flashed again and the scene broke up.

The three very young boys got up to leave. The youngest, sleepiest one managed to get to his feet but he immediately keeled forward, his face white. The marshal moved just in time to catch him and to have another pair of summer trousers ruined.

At that moment, Nesti returned but didn't risk his expensive shoes anywhere near the mess the waitress was cleaning up, only grimaced and observed, 'Thank God you're in your own car.'

'Where have you been, for goodness' sake? It's been more than twenty minutes.'

'What?'

They were forced to shout directly into each other's ears.

'Where were you!'

'Had to go out for a smoke. This place is very very correct.'

'Can we leave?'

'I think we'd better. You can get cleaned up at the hotel.'

'Hotel? What hotel?'

96

'Our next stop. Unless you want to come back another night—in which case—'

'No! Now, listen, Nesti—'

'We're in this together. You're my witness or I won't get the front page, and I'm your witness or how will you get this through the courts?'

'I'm investigating a murder, Nesti, not creating career opportunities for you.'

'It's all one. Let's get out of here. And watch out for anybody with a camera. Cristina says they like to take snapshots of anybody new as a sort of insurance policy and she thinks we might have attracted attention by trying to go upstairs with her together. That was probably a mistake . . .'

The two bouncers were escorting the star stripper from the room, clearing a path for her, delaying their departure. She was amazingly tall, like a huge doll. The marshal glanced around him. There were no cameras in sight but they could be hidden—not that it need matter to him, since he was here on official business.

It was a relief to be outside in the darkness and walking away from the noise. By the time they neared their cars they could hear their own footsteps on the gravel and the pounding music had faded to a background rhythm.

'Before we go anywhere else, what about telling me—'

'Not here,' Nesti muttered. 'It's too dark. Can't see who's around. Get in your car and follow me.'

They drove back to the town centre, to the street where they'd eaten. In front of him, Nesti signalled and turned left into an alleyway that led to a carpark. It was nothing more than a patch of bumpy spare ground, but a custodian appeared with a torch and took ten euros from each of them.

'How long is that for?' the marshal asked.

The man only shrugged and vanished into the darkness.

Back on the street, which was as brightly lit and busy as before but with fewer women about, other than young ones looking for clients, Nesti said, 'Wait there a minute. We don't want to be conspicuous again.' And he vanished into a crowded bar.

The marshal stood well away from the door, affecting to look at a four-thousand-euro handbag in one of the designer shops, but managed to watch Nesti out of the corner of his eye as he went to the cash desk and spoke to the man behind it. He was given something from under the counter. He came out of the bar, walked by the marshal without looking at him, saying, 'Follow me at a distance.'

Feeling more than a little ridiculous, the marshal did as he was told. As well as feeling ridiculous, he was tired, but he was curious too. Nesti crossed the road and turned a corner. All the buildings on the main road had been new, built from the sixties on, but now they were in a quieter street which must be nearer the spa park, judging by the smell of greenery on the night air. Nesti turned in at the gate of a liberty-style villa and stopped to wait.

'Isn't this a private house?' murmured the marshal.

'Discreet hotel.' Nesti opened the main door with a large key. There was no one in the entrance hall, no reception desk, no sign of life. Only soft lighting and huge potted plants standing on the fancy tiled floor. The staircase had an elaborate wrought-iron banister.

As they climbed, Nesti gave the marshal a key.

'We're on the first floor. Cristina will be joining me so we can carry on our little conversation, so I've paid for two rooms; so, if you want to take advantage, it's paid for.'

'No, thanks. And I hope all this is going to be worth it.'

'You'll see. Come in here. This is your room, I'm opposite. I'll fill you in a bit. It'll be an hour before Cristina gets off. Not bad, eh?'

The room was big and its centrepiece was a four-poster bed, its gauzy curtains tied back with ribbons.

'Sit down. There'll be a fridge somewhere . . .' Nesti soon discovered it, hidden inside an antique sideboard. 'Champagne . . . right—and look at that! There's even milk for breakfast! You've got to admit, Paoletti knows his stuff. Glasses are in the fridge, too. I like things done properly. Here.'

The marshal sat on a shiny striped chair and accepted the glass, though he had no desire to drink anything ice-cold at this hour.

'There you go . . . decent champagne, too. So!' Nesti plumped down on the four-poster and fished out his cigarettes. 'This is a hotel where you don't see anybody and nobody sees you. Useful for expensive love affairs; but if you haven't got a woman, Paoletti will provide. Nothing leads back to him, by the way. He owns this place, though it's in his wife's name, but what goes on here, that's the guest's business and it won't be easy to touch him for it.'

'Well, for a start, we're here and we haven't filled in a police hotel form.'

'And this isn't registered as a hotel. It doesn't look like a hotel, there's no sign outside, no reception, no concierge, no money changing hands.'

'So how did you pay?'

'At the club, but there's no record of it. I followed Cristina's instructions, went down, paid at the cash desk, and was given a number to recite at that bar in exchange for the keys. Anyway, first things first, here's how it works: I paid to go upstairs with Cristina to a private room—whole floor's about the same size as the room we were in downstairs, but divided into what you could hardly call separate rooms, not much more than cubicles, wall to halfway up and then a sort of beaded-curtain effect—I mean, if you wanted to you could peep into the next one and you can bet your life the whole lot will be under surveillance.'

'So . . . you mean you can't get up to much for your sixty euros.'

'One twenty in my case, remember—we've got to keep our accounts straight. No, you can't get up to anything at all. A bit of private lap dancing and that's it. The girls aren't allowed to do more than wriggle around and they have to keep the tanga on. So, no sex in the club, no money changing hands here. Anyway, Cristina wriggled around and we talked while she wriggled. She and another five are sex slaves. All of them came over from eastern Europe. They share a dormitory, so she knows them all. Then there are two more she doesn't know. They all came here legally to work as waitresses or in domestic service through the agency—and there are enough of them really doing that for word to have spread that it's above-

100

board. Once they're here, Paoletti looks them over and decides what to do with them. If they're not much to look at, they find themselves cleaning lavatories or looking after somebody's senile granny. They're overworked and underpaid, but they're the lucky ones. If they're pretty, all the worse for them. They end up slaves like Cristina.'

'What about the one we had dinner with? Maddalena? She's very pretty, but she's free.'

'Different circuit. Like she said, she's freelance, has a good agent. She did her stint at Paoletti's club and that was that. She can dance and somebody has to keep the standards up. Same thing with the strippers—they're real professionals, and some of them are big-time porn stars, very highly paid, also with tough agents. The poor creatures Paoletti brings in learn a few lewd poses, slither around their poles, and that's about it as far as dancing's concerned. On top of that, they're used for the weirder sorts who frequent this place. Anyway, Maddalena got talking to the other girls and told all to her boyfriend, Tommaso, who happens to be a colleague of mine.'

'Did Cristina tell you the names of the others?'

'Anna and Lara Lazurek, two sisters, Natalia, Danuta, and Maria.'

'I've seen a girl called Danuta at Paoletti's house. She really is a cleaner—what's more, she showed me her passport and work permit herself, so maybe somebody's having you on, somebody who's got it in for Paoletti.'

'Or there's more than one Danuta and the one you saw is one of the lucky ones. Besides, I've told you, they've all got legal papers, that's why he feels safe—only, in the case of the sex slaves, he keeps

101

those papers and their passports locked away.'

The marshal recognized that it might well be true. The Danuta he'd seen was far from pretty. Everything had been arranged for his visit. That was only too obvious.

'Does he harm the girls who are sex slaves? Physically, I mean.'

'Once, when they arrive. On their first night he locks them up and his bouncers are let loose on them. It's a night they don't forget. In any case, if they tried to leave their so-called jobs and run for it, where would they go? They're scared of the cops and they wouldn't get far without passports.'

'There are refuges . . .'

'Listen, there's one thing you can be sure of: Paoletti can size these girls up in seconds. If they've an ounce of spirit in them, he's on to it. It's the only time he appears at the club. He calls it auditioning.'

'Yes . . . the marshal here told me Paoletti was auditioning when he was taken ill . . .'

'And don't tell me *he* doesn't know everything that's going on here and turns a blind eye.'

'I've no evidence for that.'

'And you don't want any, right?'

'I keep telling you, I'm investigating a murder. I need to know if, being a freelance, he's trodden on the toes of the mafia, Italian or Russian. Besides, you said there were two more girls Cristina doesn't know. How come?'

'I don't know anything about the other two yet. That's why we're here. I ran out of time and, anyway, she needs persuading, she's scared of saying any more, scared of what she's already said. Have a drop more of this stuff. You're paying for it. The girls who are slaves have to be decent lookers, but they also have to be trained to satisfy some rich clients with, shall we say, particular tastes.'

'I can imagine.'

Nesti look at his watch. 'I'd better get over to my room. I'll leave you to finish the champagne—and don't fall asleep. Officially, she comes to you after me so you can talk to her. I've paid for both of us and I warn you it's expensive—these rooms can only be taken for the night—but the champagne's included, so you might as well enjoy that, at least.'

'Ugh!'

'What are you moaning about? You ought to be grateful and make the most of it!'

He left.

Once he was alone, the marshal looked about him, sipped absentmindedly at his champagne and grimaced. It was very nice, of course, but you don't want to be drinking cold fizzy stuff in the middle of the night. He placed the glass on the bedside table and stood up. Might as well see if he could do something about the stain on his trousers while he was waiting. The bathroom was done all over, floor and walls, with pretty, painted tiles. They were the sort Teresa liked, and they had a narrow strip of them in the bathroom at home. Majolica, Teresa said, and that narrow strip cost a fortune because it was hand-painted, not factory stuff. He wadded up some toilet roll, wondering at the expense of this place and the probable wealth and standing of its clients. The sink was set into a marble-topped piece of furniture with a big mirror above it. Hot water or cold? Unsure, he went for lukewarm, looking at himself in the mirror as it ran. Despite being tanned from his holidays, he looked pale. Fatigue, he supposed. A big sepia photograph was reflected behind his head showing a woman, young and plump, her soft piled curls tumbling, washing herself. As well as tired, he looked as out of place as he felt next to that picture and surrounded by all this elegance. Bull in a china shop. He sloshed at the splatter on his trouser leg, rubbed a big new cake of scented soap on it, sloshed a bit more and lifted the dark wooden seat to throw away the wad, pulling at the old-fashioned chain with a china handle. The only towels he could see had lace borders with bits of ribbon threaded through so he made another wad of toilet roll and dried the wet patch with that. Back in the bedroom, he wondered where to sit. Not on that fancy bed, that was for sure. It was all silk stuff and lace and ribbons, and there was that wet patch on his trousers to consider. So he wandered about, looking at everything as though he were at a crime scene—which, when all was said and done, it was. Not one where he'd be likely to find any evidence, though. He discovered a sort of curtained-off closet where there was a marble-topped table and everything needed to make coffee, including a fine brass espresso machine. He remembered the milk in the fridge. People did stay for breakfast, then, though not, he imagined, with the Cristinas. The sort of thing you'd need to be young and beautiful to enjoy and old and rich to afford. Well, the marshal never had been and never would be a candidate, at either end of the scale. He wished he were at home, showered and in pyjamas, between cool, freshly ironed sheets. They smelled so nice. In here it smelled of cigarette smoke, thanks to Nesti, and he could still taste the grappa that was lying heavily over his meal rather than helping digest it. Teresa would tell him off for eating so much so late: 'You know you always have nightmares.' And then she'd make him some chamomile tea and talk to him for a long time until he felt better.

He ached to go home, but the ache bumped to a stop in his chest. Teresa wasn't there. A deep sigh escaped him and he walked about, too restless to settle anywhere, opening and shutting antique wardrobes, bare of anything but coathangers, and drawers lined with marbled paper. The faint tapping at the door, when it came, was a very welcome interruption. He opened it to Cristina and let her in. She looked very different dressed in blue jeans decorated with coloured bits and sequins and a short jacket over a plain T-shirt. Little more than a child. He sat down on the striped chair and, since there wasn't another nearby, indicated that she should sit on the bed. She pulled off her jacket and, her face expressionless, unzipped her jeans.

Six

'No.'

She stopped, waiting for instructions.

'No, no . . . Sit down. I want to talk to you.'

'Like Roberto?'

'Roberto . . . ? Ah, yes. Yes, like Roberto.' He couldn't recall ever knowing Nesti's first name, though he must have seen it in the paper. He'd always known, though, that, whatever his many

105

vices, he was a real professional. He wasn't surprised that he hadn't mixed business with pleasure.

He indicated that she should fasten her jeans.

'Are you frightened'

She only stared at him.

'Do you speak Italian?'

'Yes. But will you talk slow?'

'I'll talk very slowly. All right?'

'Roberto told me to tell about the children.'

'There are children here? How many children? Two? Are they the two names you don't know?'

She shook her head. 'Don't know.'

'Have you seen them? How do you know? How old are they? I'm sorry. I'll talk slowly.'

Bit by bit they pieced her story together. She seemed to think there were two children, one about twelve or thirteen, the other much younger. They lived, as they all did, on the top floor of this building where a woman named Maria Grazia was in charge of them all.

'The one called Danuta—does she work at Paoletti's house in Florence in the afternoons?'

'No. That's another Danuta. She works there in the afternoon and washes glasses and cleans the club rooms here at night.'

'Where does she sleep?'

'She and Frida sleep in a room in the basement at the club.'

'And do they have a room in the basement at the villa in Florence too?' It would explain who was peeping out at him the other morning.

'No. Unless Frida has one now. She doesn't come here now, since . . . Danuta's not one of us, but she's scared to death of Paoletti, especially after what happened.'

'You know about that? About the murder?'

She nodded. 'Danuta thinks he killed her.'

'Paoletti?'

Another nod. 'He's got guns. Frida saw. She cleans and waits on people with Danuta, only, since it happened, he makes her stay at the villa in Florence all the time and she's scared. You won't say that I told—I mean about the guns?'

'No, no. We'll search the house and find them. We won't say anything about you or the two cleaners. Is there any other reason why Danuta thinks he killed her?'

'She's scared of him. We all are.'

'I understand. Nothing else?'

'Danuta says . . .'

He waited, not prompting, not asking. It was a while before she spoke but he held out.

'Danuta says, and Frida says, he never lets his daughters out. That's why they're so strange. And that his wife . . .'

'Yes. I know about his wife. But Paoletti didn't kill his daughter. He was in hospital.'

She shrugged, unconvinced. For her, Paoletti was all-powerful. He didn't need to be there. If he decided you were dead, you were dead. And it was a pretty good assessment of his character, too, as far as controlling his family was concerned. But a murder in his own respectable, churchgoing household? That, never. And yet hadn't he himself said it to the captain? A professional-style killing, yet something personal . . . and the wrong type of weapon. Cristina and the other girls had good reason to know how dangerous Paoletti was. He had to take her seriously.

107

'Tell me about what's happening here. About these children.'

The children, she told him, were kept separate, but the others knew they were there. They had heard them crying.

'You have never seen them?'

She held up one finger.

'One of them? Once? Where?'

'Here.' She touched the bed. 'Crying.'

If she really had seen the child, it had been for no more than a second or two. As she arrived to meet a client in the room opposite, she saw the door of this room start to open, so she shot into her room quickly, according to the rules. Never see or be seen. That would have been the end of it, but she could hear crying, so she peeped out. The man was closing the door as he left, so it was a matter of a fleeting glimpse. He was a big man, in his sixties, she thought, florid, bald dome. He pulled the door closed, but the bed, as he could see, was right facing it. She saw the child.

'You're quite sure it was a child?'

'Sure. A little child.' She indicated the height. 'Seven, eight years.'

She had closed her door then, but went on peeping through the keyhole.

'Maria Grazia went in. The kid stopped crying. That's all.'

The marshal sat for a moment in silence, working out how to move. He certainly couldn't barge up there now with only the word of this girl to go on. He'd need a warrant and he'd need to tread carefully. This was a very high-class operation, with clients to match. He could be on very dangerous ground. He would have liked to get

108

this girl, at least, out of here right now and into a safe house, but that would alert Paoletti. The children would vanish and, as Paoletti had been at pains to demonstrate to him, they would find no usable evidence. Still, Nesti had apparently done everything according to the house rules, so they could hope, for Cristina's sake, that no alarm bells had sounded.

'How long are you supposed to stay with a client?'

'Half an hour.'

'How do you get here from the club?'

'Mauro drives us. If we have to go back to the club, he waits downstairs. If not, he phones upstairs so *she* knows what time to expect us up there.'

'None of you drive, then?'

'No. We can't, because of our papers.'

'What about Danuta and Frida? They work at Paoletti's house every day. How do they get to Florence?'

'Mauro takes them. He lives in Florence with his mother. He brings them back when he comes to work in the evening. But now he only brings Danuta.'

Not since the murder, though. Nobody had seen this Mauro, but they had seen two girls leave in the mini on Saturday night. He didn't insist, not wanting to frighten her off.

'Don't you ever think of running away?'

'I have no money, no passport. If they catch you, they kill you.'

'Why are you talking to me? Aren't you afraid?'

'Because Maddalena said she'd help me. She said she'd lend me some money to start with, but I need

109

my passport. She said Roberto could fix things so that he'd have to let us go.'

'Paoletti?'

'Is it not true?'

'Yes. It's what we're trying to do.'

What else could he tell her? That he was only here because of Paoletti's daughter, and Nesti just wanted the front page? Now that he knew about the children, it was different; but, even so, Cristina was nobody's priority and she'd be the one to get caught in the machinery if things went wrong. She was too trusting, too obedient. Paoletti, as Nesti said, knew how to choose them.

'Listen, Cristina, whatever you do, don't talk to the other girls about Nesti or anything else. You have to be very careful or you'll get hurt, you know that. But don't worry about money or your passport. There's a safe house you can go to where Don Antonino will help you. You'll be able to go home.'

'I can't go home! My father will kill me! Don't send me home!'

'No, no . . . I know you think that now, but you can't imagine how worried they'll be and how glad to see you again . . .' He stopped as he saw her expression. She was looking at him as though he came from another planet. She didn't look like a child now. She looked old. He'd lost her. Her face settled behind the expressionless mask it had worn when she unzipped her jeans.

She repeated, as if to herself, 'He'll kill me.'

'No. We'll help you, do you understand? Something can be done, especially if you help us. We won't make you go back if you want to stay. Are you sure that's what you want?'

110

'There's this man, Aldo—he always asks for me. He says I have talent and that he could get me on television. He says I've got the body for it. He says a lot of the showgirls on the programme are not as pretty as me, and they're always looking for new ones. He's somebody important and another girl here got a job on a television show. It was before I came, Anna told me. She got all dressed up and went for an audition. Mauro drove her and he said she'd got the job and wasn't coming back, and she didn't either. So, now, when I get out of here—if I'm going to be in the paper like Roberto says— Aldo will see me, won't he? Do you think I have the body for it? That he wasn't just saying that to be nice?'

'No, no . . . I'm sure he meant it.'

It was true. She had the body for it. And she was very pretty, but . . .

He looked at the tired little face under its thick makeup, her limp, dark curls. He'd seen her picture in the paper a thousand times, and she was always the victim.

He looked at his watch. 'I think you'd better go. Should you muss this bed up a bit, do you think?'

'It doesn't matter.'

'This woman upstairs, doesn't she check on things?'

'Oh yes, but it doesn't matter, anyway, because it often happens with old men that they don't. She'll see those two glasses, so that's okay.' She stood up to go, but hesitated.

'What is it?'

'Can I have a drink of champagne?'

'Of course. You'd better drink from one of these used glasses, though. We can't leave three around.'

111

He filled his own glass for her and she drank it down thirstily

'Thanks. I like it on this floor because there's always champagne and nobody hurts you.'

'There's another floor of bedrooms? Apart from where you girls live?'

'That's just an attic. The floor above this one's for the weirdos, specials . . . you know . . . I'm off.'

He went towards the door with her, but she stopped him.

'I shouldn't be seen with you. It's the rule. Never see or be seen. Listen, will I really be in the paper, like Roberto said?'

'I'm sure you will.'

'So you . . . you'll be coming back?'

'I'll be coming back, Cristina. I promise you.'

Why in the world should she believe him, a total stranger, an Italian like Paoletti, a man? There was nothing much else he could say. He let her go. After waiting a moment, he went across and knocked on Nesti's door. There was no answer, so he went in.

His shoes were parked near the bed and no doubt he'd hung his fine clothes in the wardrobe. Very little was visible of Nesti himself in the tumble of silk sheets, a few locks of dark hair on the pillow, a thick hairy forearm and a Rolex. He was snoring quietly.

'Nesti! Wake up. Let's get out of here.'

Nesti mumbled something.

'Wake up, for heaven's sake!'

'Who's that . . . ?'

The marshal pulled the covers off his face and Nesti squinted up at him, mumbling, 'Oh, it's you . . .'

112

'Who else would it be?'

'For fuck's sake, Guarnaccia, go to bed. I've phoned my story in . . . it'll make the late edition . . . And you owe me one thousand eight—'

'What?'

But Nesti rolled over and was snoring again. The champagne bottle on the lace-covered bedside table was empty and, apart from the two glasses beside it, there was a balloon glass with the remains of some brandy. The marshal went back to his own room.

It was the sensible thing, after all. The rooms were paid for, it was nearly half past four, and he'd drunk a glass or two himself during the long night. He undressed and got into the four-poster. Lying there, propped on the big feather pillows, he could see out of the corner of his eye the lacey frills billowing round his head. He threw one of the pillows down to the end of the bed and lay flatter. He still felt ridiculous. Sometimes they dressed elephants in the circus in ballet frocks. Poor beasts. Did animals feel embarrassment? This bed . . .

It often happens with old men, Cristina had said. Was that just a general remark? To explain why there was no need to worry about the bed? Or did she really think that he hadn't touched her because he was too old to . . . ? No, no. She'd said 'Like Roberto.' No. Of course, he and Nesti must be pretty much the same age. All the customers here probably were. She had described a florid man with a bald dome . . . and a crying child.

He couldn't imagine falling asleep here, thinking of the floor above—were there any 'weirdos' up there now? If there were, no sound of their goings-on reached him. The ceiling was painted with clouds and, around the chandelier, pink cherubs held flowers and waved blue and gold ribbons. And above the 'weirdo' floor, in an attic, two children. Did they know each other? Comfort each other? Most probably they'd been kidnapped.

He should try to sleep, because tomorrow was bound to be a long and difficult day. He switched the flower-shaped bedside lamp off and lay there, rigid, in the dark.

An hour or so later, he was still lying there, trying to pretend he was getting to sleep. This place might not be registered as a hotel, but it had hotel noises. Things that clicked on and off and hummed. Air conditioning, maybe. He hated air conditioning. It damaged your sinuses, and if you got the draught of it on your shoulder, you could end up in serious pain. He listened to the blasted thing for a while, getting more and more annoyed, and, in the end, switched the light on and got up to look for the controls. It was definitely air conditioning because, he realized, now, it was far too cold in the room. Even the silky soft carpet was ice-cold under his feet. He searched and searched but found no controls, Of course, they'd have hidden the damn things, like they'd hidden the fridge, so as not to spoil the effect. Probably had ribbons stuck all over them or a lace frill round them. Why the devil weren't they near the door like the light switch? Things should be in their proper place.

'And that includes me, and I shouldn't be here!'

He did find the vent, at least, a cold blast coming out from under a half-moon table with fluted legs and brass decorations, and a fat lot of good it did him since there was no way of shutting it. He tried the bathroom. Nothing. He was frozen. Better get back in bed, and pull the bedclothes up round his shoulders. Could have done with a sweater. He switched the light off and, after five minutes or so, still frozen, switched it on again.

'Damn!' He got up to go to the bathroom. That was it. He made a decision.

'Nesti can do as he likes. I'm going.' He washed, dabbed a lacey towel at his dark growth of beard, scowling into the mirror, and went back in the bedroom to dress. It was twenty to six.

The night sky was just fading to grey and the damp air smelled of grass and pines. He found the spare ground where they'd left their cars. There were two others there, big, hunched, and dark. A fine shroud of morning mist gave them a ghostly, even sinister, air. The custodian was holed up in a wooden kiosk, drinking something from a plastic cup. Coffee from a flask, maybe. The marshal felt an urgent need for a coffee himself, but his need to get away from this place was stronger. His car, too, had a mist of tiny droplets on it. He nodded at the custodian as he drove past, but the man only stared at him.

Once on the motorway heading for Florence, he felt a little better. It was getting light and his eyes were scratchy with tiredness. There was no traffic and the fields on either side were white. The ring roads around Florence were still empty and smelled of trees rather than exhaust fumes. He entered the city by the Porta Romana and he was home. Coffee first, then a shave and a shower and he would start writing a report. He had to be so careful. A wrong move and those children would vanish. Go slowly, pay attention, one detail at a time.

Standing in his towelling robe in front of the washing machine in the bathroom, he contemplated two pairs of stained trousers lying on top of it. It was a fairly new washing machine, and he looked at all its rows of dials and lights and switches, frowning. In the old days when he had done his own laundry, all you did, as far as he could remember, was to stuff the washing in and switch it on. This thing looked like the cockpit of an aeroplane. After struggling for a while with cycles and loads and temperatures, spin cycle, air fluff, easy ironing, and wash and wear, he considered taking the trousers to be dry-cleaned. But no, he'd never find the time and then they'd be left for Teresa to deal with. So he stuffed them in with what was there already and switched on. Teresa had probably left it set on something suitable. He waited until a light came on. It seemed to be filling up. Then he noticed a blue plastic bubble sitting where the trousers had been. Teresa had mentioned that, but what . . . detergent. You put the detergent in that, these days. He couldn't, not now. The thing was half full of water. Well, it would all get a good rinsing, and if it didn't come clean he'd put the soap in and run it again. It was starting to trundle round. Good. One detail at a time. Be careful. He placed the blue plastic bubble neatly on the shelf above the washer, next to the detergent. There was a sheet of paper hanging there, taped to the edge of the shelf. She'd said something about that. He examined it. It was a photocopy, presumably of a page of instructions about all the cycles and so on.

And there were some handwritten notes done with a red felt-tip. 'Blue uniform shirts/coloured T-shirts socks, etc.' 'White uniform shirts/ underwear.' Well . . .

He got into uniform and went to his office.

It was still early to call the prosecutor, but he settled at his desk and made a few notes about what he needed to tell him. He needed two search warrants, for a start, one for Paoletti's villa here in Florence—unless he produced the gun or guns voluntarily—and one for the 'hotel.' But would the prosecutor—despite all his smiles and his 'your expertise' and his 'you and I know'—accept that there were grounds for either, considering he only had the word of a prostitute to go on? It needed backing up, and the only person who might be able to back it up . . .

'Don't tell me that he doesn't know everything that goes on here and turns a blind eye.'

He had to admit that Nesti was probably right. He was the only person. He might not know about the children, but he had to know about the 'hotel.' He'd said it was all above-board, but what else had he said? Something had been wrong in that conversation, something that had made him inclined to believe Nesti, but what was it? They had to have this out. He got up, checked his keys, and left the office. Going down the stairs, something that had been buried deep in his mind surfaced. It had been too soon. That was what it was. The local marshal had called him no more than fifteen minutes after the prosecutor, saying he'd been round there and done some checking, had that long conversation with the manager. He couldn't have done it in the time. He'd lied.

117

The motorway was still quiet, and by the time the sun was warming his car he was back in the spa town and following the signs to the carabinieri station.

The local man, Piazza, was standing in his quarters, in uniform, with a cup of coffee in his hand and a little girl with waist-length brown hair clinging to his legs.

'Please, Dad! *Pleeease!*'

'Your mum will do it for you. I have to get to work—and look, there's the marshal here waiting to see me.'

'He *can* see you—and, Dad, Mum never blows them up properly like you. They're always all soggy!'

'All right, but I'll do it this afternoon when we get to the pool. You don't need them now.'

'I do! I do need them now. I want to put them on now! I want to!'

'I'm sorry, Guarnaccia . . .'

'Don't worry.'

'Run and get them, then—and be quick! Her water wings. She's so thrilled with them, she wants to wear them all day. She'll not be satisfied until she's punctured them.'

The little girl scampered back with her pink and green water wings, and when they were inflated and put on she hugged her dad, smiled at the marshal, and galloped, shrieking, out of the room.

'An only child?'

'Yes. And you?'

'Two boys.'

'Let's go to my office—d'you want a drop of coffee?'

'No, thanks.'

118

Face to face across a desk, they sized each other up. Piazza, the marshal judged, was quite a bit younger than himself and this was probably his first command. His expression was open and lively, and he seemed ready to laugh at the first excuse offered. Even so, you could see he was a bit puzzled by this visit and, whether or not he had lied about checking out The Emperor, any idea that Paoletti was paying him off had evaporated before even before they sat down.

'Is it about this murder? Paoletti's daughter?'

'Yes. I went to the club last night—I should have told you, but it was unofficial and I thought I'd better not involve you in it, since your face is known here . . .'

The other man waited, still puzzled. Not being paid off, so what, then? To be so serene and cheerful. Perhaps he was mistaken and the lie had no sinister implications. He could just have been busy, thought he ought to say he'd checked the place out—after all, the prosecutor himself had called him. He could simply be lazy, though it seemed unlikely . . . so lively and energetic, all bright-eyed and bushy-tailed, the sort of colleague Teresa would think attractive. Hmph—well, there was no getting away from the fact that he'd lied. Could have misunderstood what he actually said or meant. Best just to ask him, maybe. Lorenzini would have done it. Looked him in the eyes, jabbed four fingers an inch from his nose and shouted 'Aow! What sort of story was that?' Tuscans . . . they were a race apart, that was a fact.

'Involve me in what? Are you all right? You look exhausted—you're sure you don't want that coffee?'

'No, no . . .'

'Suit yourself. So? What did you not want to involve me in?'

'It's just . . . I took a look round The Emperor—not official, as I said—not in uniform.'

'You went as a client, you mean? Undercover? Good heavens—I hope you don't mind my saying so, but you don't look a likely customer. What did you think of the place? Pretty much as I described it to you, eh?'

'Pretty much.'

'Making a fortune, I reckon.'

'Behind the scenes, perhaps. Not by charging fifteen euros entrance, including a drink.'

'No, well, it'll be more the private parties, stag nights and so on. Then there's a bit of privée stuff upstairs, lap dancing, nothing more than that.'

'Sixty euros for ten minutes.'

'Did you . . . well! Hope you enjoyed it. Must give it a try myself sometime.'

Up to now he was only amused. The thing was to uncover it all bit by bit, and watch for a change in his face. Of course, in these situations there was more than one way of paying people off. Someone who wouldn't want to dirty their hands with money might not be above a regular freebie.

'Then there's the hotel . . . the one that's not a hotel, if you follow me. Now that's more like serious money.'

'You went there, too? You *did* have a night out. No wonder you're looking tired.'

But he was still amused, not alarmed at all. Even so . . .

'Yes. What I'm thinking is that while what goes on at The Emperor can pass for being above-

120

board, that hotel can't.'

'I agree with you, but—I don't know if you've understood how it works—if we went in there, we'd find nothing but a private house, belonging to Paoletti's wife, and maybe the odd house guest.'

'And the girls in the attic?'

'Staff. Servants. And all with regular papers.'

'Yes . . . you know it belongs to his wife, then.'

'Of course. I told you, I've checked the place out—though not as . . . intimately, let's say, as you did. I'm impressed. Incidentally, I can't find out that he's treading on anybody else's toes in any way that might have caused the daughter's murder. He keeps himself to himself. Word of that would get around. He's not importing girls for any of the other clubs, I can assure you of that.'

'And can you assure me that his own girls are not slave sex labour? And that their passports are not locked in Paoletti's safe?'

There. That was where the smile faded.

'*Can* you? Isn't that what explains his profits?'

'I have no evidence for it . . . I just checked their papers. They had regular work permits for domestic labour, so . . . I'm not saying it's impossible.'

'But it's all above-board.'

'Listen, Guarnaccia—'

'No. No, no . . . I've heard what happens to those girls when they arrive.'

'Guarnaccia, you have to listen to me. Don't insist. You're investigating a murder. What's going on here has nothing to do with that murder, nothing at all to do with it—'

'You can't know that for sure. You can know he's not annoying his business rivals, whether Italian or

121

Russian. I'm not disbelieving you about that. But there could be something else, something personal. This was a very personal murder. The prosecutor on this case is not a man I've ever had a lot of time for, but even he recognizes that.'

'So investigate the girl's private life!'

'And leave Paoletti's business alone?'

The other man stood up, but the marshal wasn't standing up. He sat where he was, heavy, silent, immobile. The other looked down at him.

'I'm asking you once more. Don't insist. We'll be in big trouble, very big trouble, both of us. If you start a witch hunt, our lives will be ruined and everything here will go on as before. We'll achieve nothing. You know that's true. And people's sexual tastes, however weird they might be, are surely their own business.'

'Yes . . .' But the children? Did he know about the children? The marshal hoped not, and he wasn't going to risk telling him, because then Piazza's career could be ruined for not reporting it. There was another child in this story, after all. A little girl skipping around in her water wings . . .

'There are reasons why I have to insist—where are you going? We have to talk.'

'No. The less we talk about this, the better. And I'm not going anywhere. There's something you need to see.' Piazza took a key from his belt and opened a filing cabinet. He withdrew a large yellow envelope with 'Urgent' written in large capitals with a thick black felt-tip and sat down at the desk with it in his hands. His face wasn't bright and cheery now. He drew a sheet of paper from the envelope, hesitated, then pushed it across to the marshal with the impatient gesture of someone who'd done his best and now washed his hands of the matter.

The paper had on it a list of names. Nothing else, no addresses, just names. But each of the names was preceded by a title, whether noble or professional. It was to be expected. The marshal recognized two famous family names and an even more famous lawyer. There were two judges, a consultant physician, and a chief of police, local politicians, minor television personalities, a bishop. He stopped reading halfway down and passed the list back. Piazza blocked it with his hand.

'You need to read it all. I can see from your face that you haven't.'

'No, no . . . what's the point? It was only to be expected and, even so, I'm going to have to—'

'Guarnaccia, read the third name from the last. Or do I have to read it to you? It's the prosecutor on your case.

'So. Are you listening to me now?'

Seven

The marshal listened. If nothing else, he listened, or was silent anyway, because he didn't know what to say, where to start, and because everything that had happened up to now meant something different to what it had meant before. He needed to look at all of it again in peace but, for now, scenes were flashing at random in his head. His eyes were fixed on his colleague's face and he took in the sense of urgency and alarm in his voice, but

123

in his head he was somewhere else. He was standing in the glaring heat of a garden, waiting two hours for the prosecutor to arrive, though the August roads were empty of traffic. Where had he gone first? He was standing outside the door up in the tower with the prosecutor's hand clapping him on the shoulder as they loaded the body, fat legs and blond hair dangling, into the metal coffin. Of course he hadn't wanted to take the marshal off this high-profile case to put some clever investigator on it.

All that stuff about 'your expertise,' and all that considerate help . . . *'You have your station to run. I'll go to the hospital. I'll talk to the mother . . .'*

'Guarnaccia?'

'I'm sorry . . .' He realized that his gaze had drifted, that he was staring at the row of calendars behind his colleague's head.

'You do realize—'

'Yes . . . yes, I realize . . . I don't want to cause you trouble. I appreciate your situation.'

'What could I have done? I have a family.'

'Yes.'

'So? How are you going to proceed?'

'I have to report what I found. This . . .' he touched the sheet of paper. 'It's just a list of names. Anybody can write a list of names—where did it come from?'

'Paoletti, I presume. One of his employees must have left it here for me to find.'

'Ah. Well . . . he's very clever, very plausible. It's still just a list of names. When was this? How did you come in contact with him?'

'About two years ago, when I first took command here, he came to see me. I didn't think anything of it at the time, except that it was a bit unusual, but he was the one who initiated the contact with a really plausible story about how he always liked to be on good terms with the law because in the nightclub world nasty things could happen, even when, like him, you were trying to run a clean business, and so on and so forth.'

'And you believed him?'

'I'm ashamed to say, I did.'

'I don't think you need feel ashamed. He once convinced a priest to be a character witness for him after he'd almost beaten a woman to death, and he's had a lot of practice since then.'

'But I'm not a priest, I'm a carabiniere. Not that I didn't think it odd, as I said—but he actually came round here, all smiles and *so* respectable! And he managed to get into the conversation his donations to various charities, all of them run by the church.'

'And he brought this list?'

'No. That was later. I'd been hearing things. I mean, thousands of visitors pass through here every year to take the waters, but the actual resident population's quite small. Sooner or later, I was bound to hear stuff. I suppose that's why he got his story in first.'

'So, how did you hear? From one of his clients, I suppose.'

'Yes—not a hotel client. Those people are invisible, as you can imagine. They're either there with some young girlfriend or somebody else's wife or else they're indulging peculiar tastes. They'd hardly be likely to turn up here. No, this was a local man, a widower. A friend took him to the club to shake him out of his depression—nothing more than a bit of lap dancing. Anyway, he got interested in the girl and went back a few times. He seemed to believe she was fond of him.'

Thinking of poor Cristina, the marshal said, 'Well, perhaps she was, if he was kind to her, showed a bit of interest in her life.'

'Oh, he showed more than a bit of interest. He didn't say, but I got the impression he was thinking seriously about whether he could maybe—oh, he had no illusions about himself, didn't really expect her to stay with him. Anyway, she told him she couldn't leave, that Paoletti had her passport. She told him about the hotel, and he came to me.'

'What did you say to him?'

'What could I say? That I'd look into it.'

'And did you?'

'Yes. I went to the hotel with two of my men and we took a look round. No warrant or anything, just a routine visit.'

'And you found nothing?'

'What you'd expect. A villa owned by Paoletti's wife, a housekeeper by the name of Maria Grazia, some immigrant girls who were cleaning staff and so on, all with papers in order.'

'I suppose she didn't show you the rooms on the second floor.'

'Oh yes, she did. It was obvious she'd been instructed to. We only looked at two of them. What was the point? One was done up like a church, candles and flowers and a confessional, the other was black sheets and handcuffs, that sort of stuff. The woman opened the doors for us to look in and then shrugged. "Eh . . . Signor Paoletti . . ." As if it were a question of his own personal tastes. She was perfectly composed and, of course, we saw nothing there that was illegal. The next morning one of my carabinieri found this envelope on the doorstep.'

'And the widower? Did he come back?'

'More than once, but what could I tell him? I told him I'd keep an eye on the place, but that it would be difficult to prove a case or even get a warrant with only a prostitute's word for it . . .'

'And he accepted that?'

'No. No, he didn't. He started asking questions at the club. I warned him not to do that! I told him he was putting this girl at risk.'

'What happened to her?'

'She disappeared.'

Thinking she was going for a television audition, probably, and the body never found.

'What was her name?'

'I don't know.'

'But you know his name. He's not a prostitute; he's a witness. Another thing: this list. It's just a list. I take it people like this don't put their signature to anything. How do you know—or prove—that it means anything? That it's not one of Paoletti's tricks?'

Piazza looked down at the big yellow envelope.

'What else is in there?'

'Photographs. Not of all of them, but a lot of them. Very crude and very compromising.'

'Recognizable?'

'Yes.'

'So, there are peepholes in the bedrooms, is that it?'

'Something of the sort, I suppose.'

'And all this to keep the law off his back? Or do you think he's blackmailing them?'

127

'Your guess is as good as mine.'

'Hmph. Knowing Paoletti, there'll be a few chosen victims. He's a good judge of character.'

'Guarnaccia, just drop it. Don't insist. You'll ruin your family and mine and probably some of his victims' families, too. For God's sake—where are you going?'

The marshal had stood up.

'I have to go home . . .'

At the door, they shook hands.

'I'll do my best . . .' There was no need to say what about. They both knew he didn't mean his best to solve the case, just his best to save Piazza's skin.

And his own?

Back at the station, Lorenzini said, 'Your wife phoned—twice. Are you all right? What's going on?'

'You don't want to know. Damn . . . did she say something about going to see a flat?'

'The one you told me about, that you're thinking of buying? No. She just wanted to know where you were.'

'Hmph. Who's the woman in the waiting room?'

'Signora Nuti.'

'Ah, yes. I thought I recognized her. Don't tell me they still haven't unblocked that street drain?'

'Not a sign of them, despite the lawyer's letter—and there are storms forecast. You know how her cellar flooded last time, and she lives alone, poor soul. I can deal with her as soon as I've—'

'No. No, send her in to me.'

That was what he needed, to be back for a moment in his own world with his own people, with their small problems. He could hear his heart beating, feel every nerve end tingling at the thought of what he had to do.

'Oh, Marshal, I'm really sorry to be bothering you, but . . .'

'No, no, Signora. Sit down.'

'I don't know what else to do—I mean, it's been six months . . .'

'They're a disgrace. You've been too patient.' Easy to criticise. Teresa had called twice, and what had he done about that flat? Nothing. He'd been too busy with this case which, likely enough, would ruin their lives. Instead of worrying about getting onto the housing ladder, they could soon be worrying about his being transferred to the back of beyond. And Teresa? And the children's schools? Giovanni was enrolled at the technical school . . .

'My nephew came and helped me last time—I can't be carrying buckets of water, what with my age and my arthritis—but I can't keep asking . . .'

'No. And why should you have to?'

Whose advice could he ask without dragging them into it? Anybody he told would immediately be in the same boat. Damned if they didn't act, damned if they did.

'We'll both be ruined and things will go on here just as before.' Piazza was right.

And those children? The little girl crying on the bed?

No, no . . .

'My nephew says I should go ahead and sue, that there are so many complaints like this coming in, they don't even look at yours unless you sue. But the expense . . .'

'They'll have to meet the costs, that's not the problem. It's the time it will take, and you still in this mess.'

He had to sort the mess out before Teresa came home. She was so settled here. The children had their friends, their plans... The paper! The second edition of *The Nazione* would be out!

'Excuse me. I'm sorry, I won't keep you waiting more than a minute, Signora.'

'If you want me to come back another time...'

'No. I won't be a minute.'

She was his only link to reality, the familiar reality he could cope with, beyond which was a menacing, silent darkness. And it wouldn't be silent for long. He looked in at the duty-room door.

'I need a copy of the second edition of *The Nazione.*'

A young carabiniere was already on his feet. 'I'm going for the post, Marshal. I can get it on my way back—'

'No. Get it now and bring it to me right away.'

He went back to Signora Nuti. He wanted to keep her talking so as not to hear the silence in his head. In the end, she was the one to say she had to go and do her shopping.

'I'll do what you suggested—what was the number again?'

'Seven hundred. Don't worry, your lawyer will know the emergency order I'm talking about. It doesn't matter if you forget the number. Wait, I'll write it down for you ... here you are. And tell your lawyer he can call me if I can help. We've been round there and seen exactly what the situation is. Something in writing from us might help.'

He walked through the waiting room with her

and saw her out, delaying the moment when he was left alone with his fears, his too-loud heartbeat. What was terrible was that, no matter how hard he tried, he knew he could never be like Piazza. Whether it was the children or the other girls or what . . . The thing was out of his control and rolling forward under its own momentum. He couldn't stop it. How could anybody be expected to do this job properly? Why had he ever joined up? Why, oh, why had he gone with Nesti? Why wasn't Teresa here—

He interrupted himself to look in at the duty room.

'Don't put any calls through until I tell you otherwise.'

'Not even your wife?'

'Nobody.' She would notice something was wrong, and what would he tell her?

'Marshal? Your paper.' The carabiniere was back.

'You're sure it's the second edition?'

'Yes. I asked. Is there anything else, or can I go for the post?'

'You can go.'

He shut himself in his office and sat down with the paper.

There was a brief introductory piece on the front page with a photograph of The Emperor. When had Nesti got hold of that? Of course, he'd have taken a photographer when he went there before 'to take the waters'—when? The day they'd eaten at Paszkowski's, but what day was that? He was losing track of time. Without his usual routine, the rhythm of his daily life with Teresa and the boys, one day merged into another, a formless

131

muddle . . .

Continued on page 5.

An enlargement of that same photograph at the top and, in a box, one of the articles about Paoletti's arrest all those years ago, with a mug shot. All that mattered was the list, and Cristina surely wouldn't have known about that. She'd warned them about photographs, though . . .

He must keep calm, concentrate, read the page carefully and see how much Nesti knew—or at least guessed. But the print shifted under his gaze, and he found himself reading the same paragraph time and time again without taking in a word.

Blackmail . . . that word leapt from the page. It was only supposition. It couldn't be more than that, but supposed blackmail meant a supposed list of client/victims. What he must find was any mention of himself that would alert the prosecutor and Paoletti. He must read the blackmail part first, and he still wasn't concentrating. Suddenly, he pushed the paper aside and reached for the phone. To call Nesti and just ask . . . ? To call the prosecutor and find out where things stood, get it over with? Whatever he had in mind, the number he was dialling was his sister's. He had to hear Teresa's voice, no matter what. It was the only thing that would calm him. He couldn't tell her. She would hear that something was wrong, but he'd say he was overtired, that he didn't sleep well without her. He just needed her to talk to him so he wouldn't hear his heart beating all the time. It rang and rang. He'd apologise for not going to see the flat, promise to go, and he would go, too, and pretend to himself that things might turn out all right. But could he really cope with that? It meant ringing the bank, making an appointment with the manager, talking to the captain, fixing with the estate agent, being taken round. He couldn't make even the first move. It rang and rang. It was easy enough to deal with the people in his waiting room as though everything were normal. They presented themselves, told him what they wanted. Mostly, they just wanted him to listen. And besides, he had Lorenzini and his carabinieri to keep everything running, and he only had to be there some of the time. The station didn't stop running if he wasn't. The world didn't stop turning, but at home . . .

She wasn't there. She must have taken the boys to the beach. He let it ring until it stopped of itself, and then hung up.

Again he took up the newspaper, again tried to scan the page for his name, pushing his shoulders back to ease a painful tightness in his chest. He looked at his watch. Surely, if he'd seen the paper, the prosecutor would have called by now? No. The early editions of all the papers would have been put on his desk in the morning. He probably hadn't seen this one yet. That gave him some time. He picked up the phone again and called the paper. Nesti wasn't there, of course.

'You should try this afternoon, after three, three-thirty.'

'Thank you.'

And silence.

Then he heard a voice he recognized out in the waiting room and opened the door to save a young and inexperienced carabiniere from the clutching hand of Signor Palestri.

'I want to talk to the marshal!'

'Can't you talk to me? The marshal's very busy.'

133

'No! I want the marshal! Somebody has to do something, they have to come!'

'It's all right, son, I'll deal with it.' Guarnaccia put an arm round the tiny old man and led him to one of the waiting-room armchairs.

'Sit down a minute. Our stairs are steep and you're all out of breath.'

'Well, I am ninety-three, you know, so what can you expect?'

'You do well for your age. You always manage to come and see us.'

'To see you. I come to see you, and it's not a social visit, you know. Something's got to be done. You've got to send somebody. I'm frightened, do you understand?'

'Yes. Yes, I understand. It's a frightening world.'

'It didn't used to be like this—and if they get in, I can't defend myself. That's the point. I can't defend myself, not at my age.'

'No, of course you can't. That's what we're here for.'

'I'm ninety-three, you know.'

He lived alone, very near by. He was fearful of a world he no longer understood or had any contact with and, though he had almost no memory at all, he never forgot the marshal. They came to their usual arrangement. The marshal promised to send a squad car immediately.

'They'll be there in minutes, so you'd better get home. If they find you in, they can check inside the flat as well as the main entrance and the street.'

'Well, I'll do my best but I can't run, you know. I'm ninety-three!'

'You just walk at your usual pace. If they don't find you in, they'll take a look outside and try you

134

again next time round. You remember it worked out all right last time when you were worried?'

Since he lived so near the Pitti station, the marshal's men passed under his window in their cars frequently and this fiction of the squad car made him feel protected. Now and again he would forget and come back for the reassurance of the marshal's voice. Where else was he supposed to go?

The morning passed, a queue in the waiting room formed and dispersed, some dull paperwork imposed a sense of normality which was intermittently overwhelmed by a wave of fear flooding through him, almost stopping his breathing. He opened a file on the computer to write a report on the whole business. And just who was he going to give it to? In theory, where there was a conflict of interest concerning the Procura of Florence, the report should go to the Procura of Genoa, which had jurisdiction over Florence in such cases. The marshal knew this, but his faith in the whole system was severely shaken and no amount of theoretical knowledge could help him. They were all magistrates and he was just an unimportant NCO about to be pushed out like others had been before him. He would disappear from the scene. And if this report got into the wrong hands, so would those children.

'Follow your instinct,' was what the captain always said. 'You don't need me.' And where had following his instinct got him?

The thought of his commander, Captain Maestrangelo, intelligent, calm, capable . . . maybe . . .

The thought was dismissed in seconds. The crux of the matter was the question of the children, and

135

if he told the captain about that, then they would both be in the same boat, obliged to proceed and sure to be ruined as a consequence. How would that help?

No. He wasn't going to wreck the captain's career. There were those, the marshal knew well enough, who'd care more for appeasing the people on that list than for any number of abused children, but Maestrangelo was a good man, an honest man such as you didn't often find—and besides, if the army were to lose men like him because of the sort of people on that list, where would it end? His own career was probably finished, but how important was that in the grand scheme of things? It was only important to the marshal himself because of his wife and children. He didn't have to sit in this stupid little office seven days a week. What sort of a life was it, anyway? He could find something better to do. Years ago, hadn't Totò protested in a fury?

'Why can't you get a proper job like other people's dads!'

Well, it's an ill wind. Perhaps it was for the best that this had happened. People always said he was asleep on his feet—well, this business had woken him up, all right. Woken him up to his powerlessness, his lack of importance. He could be got out of the way the minute somebody important snapped their fingers. He'd always known it, of course, but knowing it and having it happen are two different things. A real job . . .

Anybody retiring from the carabinieri was welcome in certain types of job. Perhaps he could even earn more . . . perhaps not—and they'd have to move out, of course, right away. How much was there in the bank exactly? Teresa would know . . . and she'd said they wouldn't need that big a mortgage. But how did she know if they hadn't seen the flat and didn't know the price—or did she? In any case, if he didn't get another job immediately, there'd be no question of buying; they'd have to rent. He should go to the bank, but he was in no state to be talking to a bank manager. He was so tired, apart from the anxiety that was holding him paralyzed as he waited for the storm to break. Read the article properly, carefully, make sure his name wasn't mentioned . . . Nesti wouldn't. Of course he wouldn't. That was why they'd used his credit card last night. But that first article, the one about Paoletti's past, they'd agreed on that one, hadn't they? What happened to that? They hadn't run it the next day because of the gypsy business . . . two more children . . . there. At the bottom of the page . . . Paoletti's career, his daughter's murder and possible connections to . . .

'I give you the goods on Paoletti, you give it back to me and I write it up.'

His name wasn't there. He was just a carabiniere source. Thank God.

The prosecutor knew he was involved, though, because he'd been the one to have the old articles sent over to the Procura . . .

Too tense to sit still, he got up and told the lads in the duty room he had to go out for a bit.

'Where's Lorenzini?'

'Over at Borgo Ognissanti, don't you remember? He—'

'All right. I'll not be more than half an hour.'

Once outside, on the sweltering slope of the forecourt, he put his sunglasses on. There was

137

hardly any need to worry about his allergy to sunlight today. There was some glare but the sky was heavy and it must have started raining in some parts of the city already because you could smell it. There were storms forecast, somebody had said . . . Signora Nuti, maybe . . . poor thing, dreading every shower, dragging buckets of water up her steep cellar steps with her arthritic hands. Why was life so sad and difficult? And so frightening . . . poor old Palestri. The marshal could hardly see about him in his self-imposed gloom, but he stayed behind his dark glasses for the familiar, protective feel of them.

Some of the tourists, coming out of the Pitti palace, were struggling into flimsy transparent raincoats, the sort you buy in the street. A spasmodic warm wind whipped at their city maps so that they could neither read them nor fold them. They should hurry up and get back to their hotels—and why were they here, anyway? They'd be better off at home, safe and comfortable, instead of trailing round the world, tiring themselves out, struggling with a place, a language, a people they couldn't understand and getting wet through.

At the bottom of the sloping forecourt, he stopped at the newsagent's kiosk and bought some more newspapers and a copy of *La Pulce,* the magazine everybody bought when they were looking to buy or sell a house, a car, or second-hand funiture. He could look at the prices of flats. There was a jobs section too. And all the daily papers had one as well. He looked over at the bank, knowing he couldn't go in there. A retired carabiniere was standing outside on guard, shifting his weight wearily from one foot to the other, his face glazed over with boredom. The marshal's chest tightened at the sight. He crossed over further along and got a coffee and a sandwich in the bar. He wasn't sure whether this was elevenses or lunch because he'd lost track of time. It didn't matter. He wasn't even sure if the gnawing pain in his stomach was hunger or anxiety. The bar was crowded with people, mostly foreign, chattering loudly, as though they hadn't a care in the world. Despite their noise, he could still hear his heart pounding. It was too hot in there with so many people and the espresso machine going. Wanting to leave, his sandwich half finished, he pulled out his wallet, only to find there was no money left in it. Nesti and Lorenzini between them had cleaned him out. He stood there, perplexed. The barman caught his eye and waved at him with a hand that signalled 'another time.' He wasn't going into the bank, even so. He took a card from his wallet and walked along to the cash machine, remembering as he put his number in that Nesti had said he owed him some ridiculous sum of money. Well, it would have to be a cheque. He couldn't go into the bank.

'Storm's about to hit us,' remarked the guard, who had already retreated into the doorway. He would have liked to have a chat, that was obvious, and though the marshal didn't know him except to nod to, he felt bad about pushing the card and money into his wallet and turning away with hardly more than a grunt. The guard probably believed it was because of the nearing storm cloud. Big drops spattered his sunglasses and the newspapers as he climbed back up the slope.

The thunder began just as he started up the

stairs. His head was aching fit to burst. The lights were on.

Once shut in his office, he hung up his hat, removed his sunglasses and dried them with a big white handkerchief before putting them back in his shirt pocket. He sat down with the newspapers and opened *La Pulce* first. Shop assistants, cleaners, extra lessons, someone to look after the children, someone to look after the old, independent salespeople, must be personable.

The phone rang. Could it be Teresa? Let it be Teresa.

It was the prosecutor.

There were no polite preliminaries. The mask was off. This was the man he knew.

'This is you, isn't it?'

'I—'

'This story is by the journalist whose articles you had sent over to me. You're the source!'

'Only—'

'I understood I was running this case. You take a little too much upon yourself, Guarnaccia, and you always did. I remember you and your independent little ways. We're investigating a murder here, not helping some squalid journalist with his career!'

And how could he answer that? Hadn't he said the same himself?

It went on for a long time. It was fortunate that the marshal was given no chance to defend himself, firstly because he had no defence, secondly because it gave him time to listen to the prosecutor rather than to his words. Inevitably, though, without any feeble offerings on his part to feed the fire, the prosecutor began to repeat himself and, after that, to wind down and look for

140

an exit line. He found one. It was breathtaking.

'I've had this sort of trouble with you before, I seem to think. I remember you, years ago, hoping to save yourself a lot of work and get away to your holiday by trying to convince me that a murder was a suicide. But I was right that time and you were wrong. Just bear that in mind!'

A deafening clap of thunder right overhead accompanied the slamming down of the receiver, and a torrent of water slashed against the office window. The marshal breathed out slowly. His ear hurt, his head rang, and, even so, he felt a bit better. He hadn't heard most of the prosecutor's words, but he had heard that his anger was fuelled by fear. Not as great as his own, of course. Perhaps alarm, apprehension was more like it. Unless he was already one of those being blackmailed, he couldn't know the extent of the danger he was in. He could certainly have no idea of that yellow envelope in Piazza's filing cabinet. It was true that he, like many others on that list, could get the marshal and his colleague Piazza removed easily enough, but that didn't alter the fact that if Nesti pursued the story and the prosecutor's name came out—with or without proof—his life would fall apart. And, knowing Nesti, he would get his hands on that list sooner or later. Years ago, he'd got his hands on the P2 list and was hawking it paper to paper for ages, unable find anybody with the guts to take it on. But in the end, though Licio Gelli had gone on slipping through everybody's fingers to the last, his reign was over. This Paoletti was a similar sort of character. What made it easy for them was not just the help that money bought at a lower level and accomplices at a higher but, more

141

importantly, the fact that nobody, *nobody* wanted them in the dock and talking. Of course, Paoletti was a much lesser version. You needed a war to launch a career on the scale of Gelli's.

Alarm, then. And he couldn't say too much for fear of revealing things the marshal might not know. The people on that list were powerful and they had everything to lose, jobs, reputations, families, their whole lives. That made them very dangerous people indeed. What the marshal had also been listening for was how much the prosecutor thought he and Nesti already knew. So he needed to read page five properly.

Before starting to read, he tried his sister's number again, but there was still nobody there. He looked at his watch. Perhaps they'd taken sandwiches to the beach instead of going home to lunch. He'd try tonight at supper time. He was bound to find her then.

He settled down and started reading. Paoletti's past, he'd checked that already . . . the club that with such prices couldn't make a profit, the system with the phone numbers at the cash desk. That brought it as far as pimping. With Paoletti's history and Nesti and Piazza's widower as witnesses, the charge would probably stick. But that other girl had disappeared. What about Cristina?

He interrupted his reading to call Don Antonino at the safe house and explain something of how things stood. Don Antonino was a sensible man and experienced. He might be able to help. And it was good to talk to somebody.

'Will they know she's the one who's responsible?'

'I can't be sure; but if, let's say, Nesti was the only unknown customer in the last few days, they'll put two and two together, and if they do they can check what he looks like from the paper's website. Besides, he used his credit card.'

'We need to get her out immediately, then, but from what you say about their system of surveillance, we can get one of our helpers in there but he won't be able to get her out. Your men will have to be standing by to go in. Or even better, send one of your men in under cover in the first place. Can you arrange that? Marshal? Is there a problem?'

'Yes . . . yes, there's a problem.' But should he talk about it over the phone? Two children, locked in a room, abused and frightened to death. Poor, unimportant children. He remembered two more poor children, the ones who only became important when their small, incinerated bodies, lying in drawers at the Medico-Legal Institute, became a political football. He thought of his own two boys, healthy, happy, settled . . . until now, when he was about to spoil it for them . . .

'Hello? Marshal? Are you still there?'

'Yes, I'm still here.'

'The line must have gone dead for a moment—it must be this storm. You said there was a problem?'

'Yes, there is.'

'Do you think you might have difficulty getting a warrant? You don't believe the journalist's story, perhaps? And yet you called me. What is it, Marshal? There's no time to lose in situations like these, you know that, I'm sure, from experience.'

'Yes. You're right, of course. The problem is bigger than I said. There are . . . others in there. I have no proof but, unless I get a warrant to search the whole place the first time we go in, rather than just getting that one girl out . . .'

'The others won't be there the second time.'

'Yes.'

'But surely you will get a warrant to search the whole place? You've done this before. It goes without saying that there must be other girls but, from what you've told me about the journalist's visit, he should be able to give you more than enough evidence for a warrant.'

'Yes.'

'Marshal?'

What was he to say? On the telephone . . . was he becoming paranoid?

'Marshal? We keep getting cut off. And what with this thunder I can barely hear you anyway. Perhaps the good Lord doesn't want us to have this conversation! He probably agrees with you. It's sometimes safer not to act at all than to act hastily. Best think it over. We'll talk another day without the sound effects. Oh—now, I'm glad you called because I've been meaning to ring you about the business of that Albanian girl. I'm not sure I can keep our appointment for tomorrow. I really can't get away, I'm sorry. Would the day after be all right? Any time in the afternoon that suits you. Four? Five? You tell me when you can see me.'

'Four would be all right.'

'Four it is, then. My goodness, I can hardly hear myself speak. Is it as bad where you are?'

'Yes. Yes, it is.'

'Well, it's been far too hot. At least this will clear the air.'

He rang off.

So, he wasn't being paranoid. There was no

business about an Albanian girl. No appointment tomorrow. Don Antonino had cottoned to what was going on. There was nothing he didn't know about the world he rescued young women from.

The lights blinked and another clap of thunder rattled the window panes. It would clear the air, Don Antonino was right about that. It might even clear the marshal's head.

'But it won't clear this mess up,' he muttered, staring down at the newspaper. Well, what was done was done. He folded the paper and put it aside.

He then spent a long time composing the first paragraph of his report. It was complicated, and he was no great hand at explaining things. After twenty minutes of writing and rewriting, starting the story at one point and then another, he deleted the whole thing.

For some time he stared at the blank screen and then reached for the phone.

After three thirty, they'd said at the switchboard. He tried again, but Nesti was still not at his desk. He took up *La Pulce* and turned to the estate agents' pages. On the instant, his anxiety was fizzing in every nerve. Should he try the bank manager? Even worse. The captain? Out of the question. He'd already decided that. The flat itself, so that when he talked to Teresa tonight, he could say . . . ? No. The captain was the contact for the flat.

The jobs section. It couldn't all be about cleaning and babysitting.

It was, though—apart from personable young people between eighteen and twenty-five to work in publicity—meaning ringing doorbells and putting advertising leaflets into people's postboxes. Pages and pages of dead-end jobs, most of them clearly aimed at illegal immigrants willing to do what nobody else was prepared to do for wages nobody else would accept. He turned the page. This looked better.

Expanding business, Florence, seeks qualified personnel.

Delivery boys, warehouse staff, office staff, also part time . . .

Immediate employment! Sign on to one of our free courses . . . few places still available . . . secretarial work—computer studies—English—Spanish—Italian . . .

'Italian? Ah . . .'

If you are an unemployed non-European immigrant with valid permit . . .

'Hmph.'

Pizza delivery—must have own moped . . .

Barman with experience in hotel work . . .

Well-established detective agency! Minimum age 30, for investigative work, telephone interviews national and international correspondents. Good business background, excellent computer skills, English, dynamic personality . . .

What, after all, did he know how to do? What could he offer? He could just about manage one programme on the computer. What else? He couldn't think of anything.

He wouldn't qualify for even the humblest of jobs that the poorest immigrants did.

He thought of Teresa looking after his mother all those years. Nobody would do that now. These days somebody from the Philippines did it.

Earn up to 800 euros a month part time. Choose

146

your own hours.

18–25 yrs, must be personable . . . sales experience.

That eighteen-to-twenty-five line cropped up a lot. Eight hundred euros, evidently on commission, no fixed salary. And, in any case, how could anyone live on 800 euros a month? A lot of people paid that in rent. Perhaps he should be looking at flats for rent instead of wasting his time . . .

The thunder was more distant now, but the rain went on beating heavily against the windowpanes and it was getting darker and darker. It was still hot and sweaty in the little office, but he shivered, thinking of all the sad people out there in the wet, looking for work, however badly paid, for a permit to stay, for somewhere to live, for some way to get a foothold on life . . .

Whilst he had all of it, everything his poor peasant father had wanted for him, a solid, comfortable home, a good, steady income, a wife and family, security, respectability, everything. And he was about to put it all at risk.

Eight

This time he typed a page and a half of his report before deleting it. It wasn't clear. There was no proper sequence to it. He wasn't much good at this anyway, but today he was so tired . . .

Tired or not, there was no time to lose. The fear that anything he did and anything he didn't do, anything he wrote or didn't write, might spell disaster for those children blocked him. But he would do it. He had to do it. The thought of those

147

rich men with particular tastes . . . he couldn't abide that sort of thing . . . a seven-year-old . . .

'Your little independent ways.'

Was it arrogance? Was that what made him think he knew what should be done, what could be tolerated and what couldn't? He wasn't conscious of it, but that didn't mean anything. Who was he to decide what other people should or shouldn't do?

'The Tyrant of Syracuse!'

His sister, Nunziata, had called him that. She was laughing at him when she said it, so she was only joking . . .

'You always had to be the boss.' She wasn't joking. He'd decided for her where she should convalesce, mobilizing his contacts in the hospitals here without even bothering to consult her.

'Your little independent ways.'

It was only because he was worried about her. He hadn't meant any harm. Teresa, at least, understood, didn't she?

'But what if she doesn't want to?'

He hadn't consulted Teresa either, though, had he? And who was supposed to nurse Nunziata through her convalescence? The same person who'd nursed his mother. How dare he even suggest it? What gave him the right to make a decision like that? Being a man? And then the women in the family took the consequences and did the donkey work. How could he have dared . . .

And it wasn't the first time she'd faced him with it.

'You spend all day ordering those poor lads around and then you come home and start . . .'

What had it been about, that time? He couldn't even remember; but, even so, the words might have been burned into his brain, they came back to him with such clarity. He could hear her voice saying them, as though she were in the room.

Wasn't he supposed to give his carabinieri orders? Didn't he do his best for them? He'd thought he was doing his best for Nunziata too . . .

In the heat of his agitation, he got up, frowning, and went to the door of the duty room. Two faces looked up at him, waiting for his command.

When he only stood there in gloomy silence, they exchanged the briefest of glances and stood up, looking puzzled.

The senior man said, 'At your orders . . .'

They waited.

'No, no . . . carry on. I was just wondering . . .'

What had he wanted to say to them? Do you think I'm a tyrant?

'Isn't Lorenzini back?'

'Not yet.'

'Carry on.'

As he withdrew, he heard them murmuring.

'What's the matter with him?'

'Bad-tempered because his wife's away . . . so, go on. What did she say?'

'Wait. That's the patrol car. One one seven. Come in, one one seven . . .'

Back in his office, the marshal felt so wretched that he turned to the computer, hoping that anger and irritation would override his feeling of shame as he wrote the daily orders for tomorrow.

Somehow or other, he had to get through the rest of his day and then go back to his quarters and call Teresa. He would apologise. He would let her decide what to do about Nunziata.

But he didn't get the chance. At half past eight,

149

when he was showered and changed, she still
wasn't there. He sat with the portable phone in
front of the television with the sound turned off,
calling and calling, and each time that he gave up
and rang off, he imagined her coming in the door
at that very minute, missing the call, and he'd try
again.

But still it rang and rang, and in his mind he
pictured it ringing on that low cupboard thing in
the darkened entrance. Where were they?

Picnic lunch at the beach and then out to
supper? They were having a fine time of it while
he was struggling here! They could have been
invited by Nunziata's friends from the flat
opposite. Teresa had mentioned them the other
day . . . Di Luciano . . . the children played
together so—well, he hoped to goodness that was
the case and that they weren't out wasting money
in some pizzeria with all the financial worries he
had now. The gnawing pain gripped his stomach
again

The phone rang.

That must be her! And about time! Forgetting all
about his apology, he picked up and answered in a
temper.

'Hello!'

'Guarnaccia? Nesti.'

'Oh . . .'

'What's the matter with you?'

'Nothing.'

'Tired, I suppose—I told you to get some sleep.
What was the big hurry to get home to an empty
house? I had a good long sleep—and then I paid
a little visit to your colleague out there. Piazza.
He—'

150

'What did he say?'

'To me? Nothing, as you can imagine. I'm surprised you didn't go round there. He might have talked to you. He looked scared to death, though, so he knows plenty. I told you he would.'

'Leave him alone, Nesti, please.'

'This story's big, very big. And he knows all about it, believe me. If you'd seen his face this morning—'

'Nesti—'

'Is he a friend of yours? Is that it? Or someone you owe?'

'No.'

'Just protecting our own, then. Didn't Cristina tell you about the children—'

'Leave him alone—at least for the moment. Please.'

'For the moment? You've got something, then, have you? All right, listen: I'll leave him alone for the moment—but keep me informed. I mean, if this thing's going to break, big-time, I want to be the only journalist there.'

'When are you not the first one on the scene?'

'Not the first one on the scene, this time, the *only* one on the scene. And it's not going to be that easy, now that the story's out. I've been straight with you, remember, I didn't mention your name—even where you'd agreed to it in the part about Paoletti's past.'

'Hmph.'

'What does that mean?'

'It means you didn't need to. Carabiniere source . . . who else could it have been? The Paoletti case is mine.'

'What is the matter with you? I should have

151

thought you'd be grateful. If I hadn't turned up that background stuff on Paoletti, where would you be with your case?'

'Nowhere.' Where he'd like to be. He was being unfair. Nesti didn't know about the list in Piazza's filing cabinet, though he was smart enough to guess something of the sort was likely to exist—in which case he ought to be treading more carefully and not just thinking about his own . . .

There he went again! Now he was deciding how Nesti should do his job, run his career. Who was he to criticize? Nesti was a very experienced journalist—and he, at least, still had a career in front of him. He was doing himself some good, while—

'Guarnaccia?'

'What!'

'Oh. I thought the line had gone dead.'

'No.'

'But I take it you're not overwhelmed with enthusiasm about my interview, even though I did keep your name out of it—I hope you approved of my tie, at least. Hand-woven raw silk. I bought it specially.'

'Tie . . . ?' There was no interview in the paper! *'Tie?'*

'You didn't even see it, did you? I'd have called you to tell you to switch on, but I didn't have a minute.'

'You've done a television interview? About this case?'

'Only on the regional news at half past seven on three, but it'll be picked up by the national news tomorrow, you'll see.'

'Nesti . . .' What was the use? The thing would

152

take its course. He'd felt all along that he couldn't control it. He ended the conversation and sank back against the coolness of the leather sofa, staring at the silent flickering of the television, still clutching the phone. He forced himself to concentrate on the images on the screen, trying to make sense of them, promising himself to follow this film, or whatever it was, until there was an advertising break. Then he'd try Teresa again. She had to come in sometime. The boys shouldn't be out too late, holidays or no holidays. They were still growing. They needed their sleep. She really ought to—No! He was doing it again. What about criticizing himself, for once, since he'd failed to get anywhere with his report and had been forced to give up out of tiredness. Concentrate on the television—another thing he was incapable of, according to Teresa. Was that the man in the antique shop? It was. The other man was terrified of him. You could tell just from looking at his face how his stomach was tightening till it hurt and he wasn't breathing properly. In sympathy, the marshal tried to take a deep breath for him, but all the sympathy in the world couldn't help him to follow the story. It wasn't his fault, because he'd missed so much of it when he was on the telephone. They were quarrelling now, the frightened man and his wife, shouting, you could tell by their mouths and their attitudes. But how was he to supposed to follow it? He couldn't hear a thing they were saying.

'Oh, for God's sake!' He zapped the sound back on and immediately zapped it off and tried Teresa again. Nothing . . . nothing . . . nothing . . . nothing. Damn!

But almost on the instant he tossed the phone aside, it started ringing. She'd come in the second he'd rung off, just as he'd imagined!

'Guarnaccia?'

'Mr. Prosecutor. Good evening.'

The call only lasted a few minutes and apart from an obligatory 'Yes, Mr. Prosecutor' here and there, the marshal said nothing.

When it was over, there in the semidarkness, he sat still for a long time, not thinking, his mind in neutral. Random thoughts, irrelevant, disconnected, surfaced and vanished, the way they do when you're falling asleep. He hadn't done anything about that stuff in the washing machine. It must be nice to have a little girl who thought you were the only person who could blow up water wings properly. That wasn't the frightened man's wife. The woman who worked in the antique shop maybe . . . blonde. Credits. It must be later than he thought. Had he eaten . . . yes, a sandwich in the bar . . . or was that . . .

He went on sitting there because if he moved, connected up to reality, he wouldn't be able to cope.

But even as he sat there, the poison that had entered his ear was working its way through his system. He felt cold.

His voice had been quite different this time, the tone of it. Last time, it had been high-pitched with annoyance and apprehension; now it was low and insinuating and full of menace.

'Some of these people have a great deal of power and no scruples.

'You know well enough what the risks are.

'Nothing more than a witch hunt, when all's said

154

and done. A journalist is one thing but in your own interests.

'*People with a great deal of power and no scruples would crush you.*

'*It goes without saying that I'll do what I can to protect you.*

'*From one day to another, to wake up and find yourself posted to some desolate village at the end of the world.*

'*You don't deserve it, your family doesn't deserve it.*

'*Come to my office tomorrow and we'll talk about what can be done for you.*'

Drop by drop the poison seeped through him, and his only reaction was to think he was very, very tired. And so he got up and walked through the flat, locking up, closing shutters, leaving the windows open for the night air. It hadn't rained enough, even now. The heat was steamier than before and there seemed to be more mosquitoes. He went to bed and fell asleep as his head touched the pillow, but it was the tense, superficial sleep of a guard dog. A breath would have woken him.

*　　　*　　　*

When he opened his eyes it was still dark. He remembered no dreams. His head was clear. There was no need, as sometimes happens, to wait for realization, for the cause of the pain squeezing his chest to come to the surface. It was as if a part of him hadn't slept at all but only waited for the rest of him to wake up, ready to act. It was half past four in the morning. He got up and made the bed. Washed, shaved, and in uniform, he stood and looked at himself in the bedroom mirror as though at a stranger. And if he never wore this uniform again? Who would this person in the mirror be then? Hundreds of people knew him as the marshal, but how many people knew him as Salvatore? 'The marshal' would be whoever took over from him. People soon got used to a new face; he would be forgotten. All that was going to happen was what must happen anyway when he retired, so what did it matter?

He wouldn't accept a posting to 'some desolate village at the end of the world.' He would find a way to keep his family here where they were happy, where Teresa was settled and the children had a good choice of schools.

On his way to the kitchen to make himself some coffee, he looked at each room in his quarters as though for the first time. It was very nice, of course, spacious and comfortable, but it wasn't his own, was it? Teresa was right. They had to think about the future.

He put the coffee on and waited for it to percolate. The army used up your life and then you were on your own. That was the way it was.

He drank his coffee standing in the kitchen with the window and outer shutters open. The Boboli Gardens brought a lot of dampness. Oxygen, too, though, and the sawing of the crickets on summer nights which had once been the sound of his loneliness now seemed one more part of a life that was slipping away from him.

Well, it was sad, but there were worse things. Beaten women and abused children, for example. And besides, the army didn't own the Boboli Gardens. There were hundreds of flats overlooking them. He closed the shutters with a bang, rinsed his cup, and went to open up his office.

It was cool in his little room at this hour. The computer behaved itself. He typed for more than an hour without stopping. He didn't try to make a work of art of the thing, connecting facts and ideas. He just started his story on the nineteenth of August and went on until he got to today. What difference did it make if he couldn't make a convincing, logical case? If somebody wanted to hear what he had to say, they would listen and act. If nobody wanted to hear . . .

He had left a space at the top, not knowing exactly whose name to put there. The Chief Public Prosecutor of the Republic, Genoa? Probably. But there might be someone in particular who dealt with conflict-of-interest cases. And what if there was? He would still know nothing about the man. What might his sexual habits be, for a start? And he might even be great friends with one or both of the judges on that list, even with the prosecutor on this case. When all's said and done, people protect their own, as Nesti said. Wasn't he himself protecting Piazza?

The report was complete, but the address line remained blank. There was nothing to be done; he must ask the captain. If he didn't know the answers to these questions, he was, at least, in a better position to find out. The marshal would neither ask him nor tell him anything else about the matter. He printed the report, put it in an envelope without sealing it, and filled in a registered-letter form which he attached to the envelope with a paper clip.

Then he opened a new file and wrote a letter to

157

the General Command of the Carabinieri:

I, the undersigned, Salvatore Guarnaccia, born in Noto in the Province of Syracuse on 16th . . .

If he hesitated there, it was only to do a quick calculation of his years of service. Would he be entitled to any part of his pension at all? The captain would help with that.

Marshal major in the service of Regional Command, Tuscany, request permission to take early retirement from 26th October of the current year. I intend to be domiciled . . .

Where? He was obliged to give an address, and he didn't have one.

I intend to be domiciled . . .

It couldn't wait. He must resign before he could be transferred, and he knew from experience that it could be a matter of days. Finding a house could take months. More than the three months' notice he'd had to give.

I intend to be domiciled in Noto, provincia di Syracuse . . .

He gave his sister's address. He would go home.

Florence, 26th August . . .

He printed, signed, and put it in an envelope. It had to be delivered by hand to his commanding officer. He would walk over to Borgo Ognissanti now. He glanced at the window. It was light. He switched his desk lamp off and stood up. The walk would do him good, and he'd be back well in time to open his station.

Outside, he looked at the expanse of damp forecourt in the sickly, pinkish light. There wasn't a soul in sight. Not so much as a dog. He walked down the broad slope and crossed the empty road. All the metal shutters were down. Sdrucciolo de'

158

Pitti was so narrow, its buildings so high, that it was still almost dark there. His footsteps echoed in the alley with its uneven paving stones. A small black cat appeared from the deeper shadows of a doorway, walked with him down the alley in silence for a while, and then slid behind a grating and vanished. He turned right, made for the river, and crossed the Santa Trinita bridge. Without traffic, the smell of the river was strong, but he didn't glance down at the level of the water the way he usually did, only walked on at a steady pace until he reached the barracks in Via Borgo Ognissanti.

'Morning, Marshal.'

If the young guards on duty were surprised to see him at that hour, they made no comment. He passed in his letter to the captain at the window, nodded, and walked away.

It was done. Going back, his walk was slower and he was breathing more easily. It was still very early as he walked upriver towards the Ponte Vecchio. The sun was up now, the pearly pink sky turning blue above the dark olive-green water. He had always liked to walk by the river. He and Teresa, years ago, had taken a walk like this most evenings after supper, stopping to sit in that little garden on the left bank to chat and look across at the floodlit towers and palaces on this side. How long was it since they'd done that? At some point, it had stopped being a pleasure . . . too much traffic noise and exhaust fumes. There was a traffic block on summer nights nowadays, but they'd lost the habit. So many years . . .

Pausing on the Santa Trinita bridge, he thought about those years, gazing upriver at the tumble of overhanging windows of the oldest bridge. The Florentines . . . they were a funny lot, but you had to hand it to them. It looked so lovely on this quiet morning.

A boy, coming towards him on a moped across the bridge, ripped into the silence and his thoughts with a fierce roar. The youngster, enjoying having the city to himself, did a couple of wheelies before he noticed the marshal and dropped his front wheel. Well, he'd no doubt have done the same at that age if he'd been given a moped. The noise faded. He'd complained a lot over the years about that noise, about the muggy climate, the smelly, medieval drains, the streets clogged with tourists, the baffling character of the Florentines. And now the place had . . . well, he'd got used to it. That must be what it was. In any case, he had to find work here. The captain would help him. He knew a lot of people, had some influence.

Well-established detective agency . . . excellent computer skills, dynamic personality . . . what a thought!

As he turned to walk on, he saw his first Japanese tourist of the morning, taking photographs of him against this famous background. No accounting for tastes.

He reached the Palazzo Pitti and turned left to where the huge iron lantern hung from the stone archway leading to the entrance of his station. How many times had he—oh, for goodness' sake! It was the entrance to the Boboli Gardens as well, and he could go in as often as he wanted.

At this hour, though, he needed his electronic key to open the gates that closed the archway off until the gardens opened. As he reached the foot of his staircase, one of the garden custodians in the glass cubicle on the right waved at him to stop.

'I think this must be for you.'

He pushed an envelope through the window.

'For me? There's no name on it.'

'No, but it says urgent. We found it propped against the gate when we arrived about ten minutes ago, and it's not for us . . .' He glanced at the other custodian, a young woman who reddened a little and turned away.

The marshal felt his heartbeat quicken and his whole body heat up as he took the thing.

'Thanks . . .'

He started up the steep stairs. He was breathless, but it wasn't because of the climb. There was nothing except 'urgent' written on the envelope with a broad felt-tip in block capitals. It was large and yellow.

Lorenzini appeared as soon as he unlocked the door.

'Your wife called to say—'

'Later. I don't want to be disturbed.' He shut himself in his office. It was something if Teresa had remembered his existence. He'd call her when he could. He'd spent enough time waiting, listening to a phone ringing in an empty flat.

The yellow envelope lay on the desk before him. He turned it over. It was unsealed. *This must be for you.*

That young woman's embarrassed face.

Some sort of anonymous threat. If it was, it couldn't touch him now. He had resigned. It was over.

He opened the envelope.

The photograph was an A4 computer printout.

He drew in a sharp breath and his heart thumped.

'*This must be for you.*' Of course, the garden custodians had opened it. And there he was, his face expressionless, eyes red in the light of the flash, and behind him . . .

The stripper was stark naked. She was bent over with her back to the camera, legs spread, peeping round. His head was between her calves.

It was a trick. It looked as though he were sitting on the edge of the stage right at the stripper's feet; but he had never been there, never moved away from his seat except to leave. Of course . . . the mirrors. The stripper was reflected behind him. At the bottom left of the picture was part of an outstretched hand, blurred as though it were moving, but definitely a woman's hand with red nail varnish. Right down in the corner was a bright orange semicircle. Part of the peak of a baseball cap.

'*Take a photo of me with your camera! Go on . . . another . . .*'

'Hmph.' Well, he wasn't going to try and explain that away to the gardeners. They could carry on giving him funny looks until the whole story came out—which wouldn't be until those children and young girls were safe. He would have liked to screw up the picture and throw it away, but it was evidence. He took a folder from his drawer and slipped the printout into it.

He thought of calling Nesti, and then thought not.

To discredit the source was the classic way of killing an accusation. The photograph was the start of it. It was unfortunate that his resignation would look like a confirmation that he was in the wrong, but it couldn't be helped. Perhaps he needed a lawyer. He thought of all the lawyers he had known through various cases, but none of them inspired him. There was time, anyway. He wasn't going to tell this story to anyone until his resignation had been accepted and the Procura in Genoa had received his report. Once he'd spoken to the captain and was sure he wasn't making a wrong move, he could transmit the thing by E-mail as well as by registered letter. There was no time to lose, as Don Antonino had pointed out. Nesti, he could rely on to keep his word. Piazza, trapped now between a rock and a hard place, would keep his head down; and Maddalena was probably the sharpest of all of them. She would keep quiet now and be an impressive witness later. The only weak link was Cristina, but one weak link was enough . . .

There was a tap at the door. The face that looked in was that of his youngest recruit, the one he'd saved from old Signor Palestri.

'What is it?' The marshal placed his big hand on the folder with its photograph at the sight of his fresh young face.

'Excuse me, Marshal, but I was told not to pass any calls through to you and there's someone who says you told him to telephone about a seven hundred order. I'm sorry, but I thought you should decide if it's urgent, because I don't understand what—'

'Signora Nuti's lawyer, is it?'

'A lawyer, yes.'

'All right. Put him through.' Poor Signora Nuti. After that storm . . .

The man seemed to be on the ball, at any rate.

163

'You know how these things go, Marshal. The judge could all too easily turn it down and order only damages, which is useless in this instance since it's the cause we need to get at. We can sue for damages once that's removed, but I need a strong case now for an emergency intervention. The signora says your men have been there and can vouch for the blocked street drains being the cause.'

'I'll see that you get a written statement to attach to your application.'

The man seemed genuinely concerned.

'There'll be a question of moral damages, too. She has terrible arthritis, and if she slips on those wet cellar steps . . .'

'I hope you can persuade her not to go anywhere near the cellar. I've tried, but she's afraid for the foundations of her house.'

'Of course she is—and, let's face it, Marshal, it's all very well to tell her not to try carrying buckets herself. But unless there's somebody else to do it . . .'

A good man. Perhaps he should make an appointment with him. Without going into any detail, he could, at least, set out his general situation. There'd be no limits to how far the people on that list would go to discredit him. The photo was only a warning shot. There might well be one of him undressed in that hotel bedroom, too. He might feel better at the thought of somebody knowing, being there to advise him as things developed. Should he ask?

'You've been an enormous help, Marshal.'

'Don't mention it. Now, there's something I have to—'

'Oh, I'm sorry, I shouldn't be keeping you on the phone over this when you must have so many bigger problems to deal with.'

'No, no . . . it's just that I—'

'I do apologise,' continued the lawyer, 'but, to tell you the truth—though I'm reluctant to take up more of your time—I had in mind to ask you about another matter that you'd be just the right person to advise me on.'

'Ah,' said Guarnaccia.

'I only take civil cases myself, but my nephew's a criminal lawyer, and under the new system he needs someone to do investigative work, checking alibis, statements, and so on—I just thought you might be able to suggest somebody—without going to any trouble—I wouldn't dream—but perhaps a retired colleague you could recommend.'

'I . . . it's possible that there is somebody. Leave me your number.'

He wrote the lawyer's name and number in his pocket notebook.

It would have been a waste of time asking, anyway, if he only took civil cases. There was no knowing what he might have to defend himself against. And the nephew? There was nothing to stop him having a talk to him. Getting more information about this job. It was worth doing in itself, but it would also give him a chance to size the man up, judge whether he might be the right man to defend him if needed.

He tried to push this thought aside and concentrate on dealing with the people who were now starting to appear in the waiting room. He sent them all away satisfied, or, at least, calmer, only to find that the thought of that lawyer had never left him and that he was going after that job and getting it before he had to tell Teresa he'd resigned. It would all turn out all right. It would be more than all right. They'd all be better off.

He pulled out his notebook and dialled the number. The man must surely have been surprised, but he was certainly delighted.

'I can't tell you how grateful I am. I'll ring down right away and tell him to expect you. We're in Via Por Santa Maria right opposite the porcellino. Francesco's on the second floor, directly below me. His name's on the door. I do appreciate this.'

After such a long, cool start to his day, the wall of heat outdoors came as a shock. Sheltered behind dark glasses from the oppressive sun, he pushed his way through the tourists on the Ponte Vecchio, wondering, for once, not why they came here but whether it wouldn't be nice to be one of them, to enjoy all the attractive things, the paintings, the architecture, the fine gold work in these tiny shops, the food. And then just get on a plane and leave, escape.

He had never set foot in one of the jeweller's on the bridge, and in all his years here he had probably not visited even half of the museums. And they rarely ate out. Well, it was going to be different now. He would have a real job that even Totò would approve of, with regular hours, weekends away, a life like other people had.

A breeze touched his burning face and, above the river, an enormous white cloud was moving. The sort Teresa called whipped cream.

The straw market was busy and, beside it, the porcellino was surrounded with people rubbing the boar's shiny bronze nose and dropping pennies

166

into the water for the orphans. What would happen to those two children? Now, that was the man to help! What was his name? The one who'd placed the little Albanian girl in the country after her pimp had her thrown out of a car on the motorway . . . he had been a children's judge. If only he were on this case, how different things would be.

He rang the bell of the legal office and the door clicked open. Second floor . . .

The lift was engaged. He pressed the bell and waited. When it came down, two men wearing short-sleeved shirts and carrying briefcases came out in a waft of perfume, deep in conversation. One of them held the lift door open for the marshal.

'Thank you.'

He got in and closed the doors on himself. It was a small lift, and it smelled strongly of the men's perfume and old varnished wood and whatever that linoleum stuff was at his feet. He raised his finger to the button marked two and felt a sickening drop in his stomach as though the lift had set off at high speed. What was he doing here? This wasn't real, it couldn't be! He couldn't press the button. Beads of sweat formed on his forehead. He pulled the inner doors open and pushed at the outer one. He would phone, cancel the appointment. He had to get home. He made for the bridge. Home. He wanted to take a shower, see and touch his own things, feel the coolness of the leather sofa, rest in the quietness of a shuttered room. Despite the heat, he quickened his pace, or tried to. Sauntering tourists on the bridge bumped into him, blocked his way with

167

wide carrier bags from the fashion shops, framed rucksacks, big cameras. On the other side, hot wafts of pizza dough, peppers, and herbs awoke hunger and loneliness. Here and there, shopkeepers greeted him.

'Morning, Marshal.'

He was almost home. When he got there, he went straight to his quarters. Bracing himself for the silence of the clean, bare kitchen, he opened the door.

'Oh, so there you are! What in heaven's name is going on?'

'Teresa . . . ?'

Nine

'I'll "Teresa" you! And don't you tell me Lorenzini didn't tell you to pick me up at the airport. Nearly an hour I waited for you, and then had to wait for a taxi in this heat—but don't bother to tell me what's going on! I've nothing better to do than fly up and down the country running after you instead of looking after people who really need me—and don't just stand there staring—just what is the matter with you?'

He followed her as she swirled into the kitchen like a tornado. The light was on in the shuttered room and there was stuff everywhere, cupboards open, a basket of washing. Her voice was angry, but it was her voice. She was home.

'Flying up and down . . . ? You're going back . . . ?'

'Of course I'm going back!'

'And how much is that costing? We're going to have to be more careful now that—we can't afford this! And where were you last night? We can't afford all this eating-out business either!'

'Eating out? So that's it—I was wondering what this was about.' The fridge was wide open, emptied. She thrust a small pan under his nose. He stared at it and at the curl of dried reddish-brown crust inside without understanding. 'It's nice to know you've been enjoying yourself eating in the best restaurants in Florence while I've been—'

'Restaurants? I've been working night and day, I've had no sleep—'

'Oh, I can see that. That would account for all those restaurant bills on the chest of drawers in the bedroom and two pairs of trousers ruined with wine stains.' She slammed down the pan and held up a pair of trousers in each hand. The wine stains were still there, pinkish now, but the trousers looked small and had blue streaks on them.

'What have you done to them?'

'What have *I* done to them? Oh, for God's sake, Salva.' She rolled them up and stuffed them into a half-filled rubbish bag. 'Brand-new—a beautiful summer wool! What were you thinking of? And stop staring at me as though you'd never seen me before— Do you even know what day it is?'

'Of course I know what day it is! Do you imagine I can run a barracks and not know what day it is? Don't talk to me like that!'

'Don't you dare be angry at *me!*'

'It's not you I'm angry at!'

'Well, there are only two of us here!'

'I'm . . .'

'Salva, do you know what day it is, or not?'

Why was she asking him that? Why? Blindly he groped through the family calendar of birthdays and anniversaries, but it was no use, so he only muttered 'Tuesday . . .' That much was on the daily orders, that much he was sure of.

'And? I can't believe you! You've actually forgotten that they operated on Nunziata yesterday? And not a word from you, not so much as a telephone call to ask how she was. Don't you have a thought in your head for anybody but yourself?'

'I did call. Yesterday. I don't know how many times.'

'Salva, I *told* you I'd be at the hospital all day and that if they let me, I'd stay the night.'

'But . . . there was nobody, not even the boys . . .'

'They slept at the Di Luciano's in the flat opposite. I told you . . . And I told you that when I was home, I'd call you so you could call me back. You know I can't have a mobile phone switched on at the hospital, but you never *listen* to me. I don't know what to do with you . . .'

She was winding down, but he was sorry she was. A senseless quarrel was better than a serious talk, a real explanation. He couldn't tell her. He would tell her about the restaurants and the trousers, but he couldn't tell her he'd resigned.

She turned her back on him and started washing the little pan, rinsing it, washing it, rinsing it, over and over, her movements furious.

He remembered the tomato sauce, now, with the leaves of basil left whole. He remembered that there were some other things, favourite things, that she'd prepared and left in the freezer.

'*Remember to take out what you want the night*

170

before.'

They were still there, untouched.

He moved close behind her and put his arms around her. She went on washing and rinsing the clean pan, her body stiff, resisting him. He bent his head to breathe in the smell of her hair.

'Is she all right?'

'She'll be fine. She'll have to have a check-up every so often, but she doesn't need chemotherapy. They caught it very quickly. Lorenzini said . . .'

'What?' He rested his cheek on the top of her head. She was softening against him. 'What did Lorenzini say?'

'He said there was something wrong with you. He was afraid you might be ill. He said he couldn't get a word out of you and that you didn't look well. And he said—'

'You've been spending a lot of time chatting to Lorenzini.'

'Well, I could never find you. Besides, he was worried about you. You're not really feeling ill?'

'No.'

'Then what?'

'It's . . . I've had some really big problems with a case . . . serious problems. I tried and tried to call you and talk to you, but—'

'A case? All this upset's about a case? Salva, I know how much you care about your job, how important the army is to you, even if you grumble and pretend it's not, but . . .'

Her words cut him like razor blades. She turned in his arms and looked up at him.

'Can't you just do your best and leave it at that, like other men do?'

171

'I *do* do my best.'

'But you always get so upset! You can't save everybody, you know. And look where it's got you this time. You've got everybody worried, even Lorenzini—and he's not one to take any notice when you get in one of your states.'

'What states?'

'You've upset me and got me rushing up here when I should be looking after Nunziata—and she doesn't even know you've never asked about her. I had to pretend I'd talked to you and that you sent your love and were thinking about her.'

'I *have* been thinking about her. But I thought she thought I—I thought she was annoyed with me for interfering, and you too. After what she called me.'

'After . . . you're not serious? That was a *joke,* Salva.'

'No, no. She was right. I've no business to be deciding everything, controlling everybody's lives. It's women who do all the work, and men just make a nuisance of themselves.'

'What?' She pulled back, staring up at him in alarm. 'Are you sure you're all right?'

'No. I'm not all right. And it's not true that I only care about my job, either—and I certainly don't care about the army. You're wrong about that. I'm tired of it, all of it. Totò's right.'

'Totò? What's Totò got to do with it?'

'He said I should get a proper job.'

'When did he say that?'

'Oh, years ago . . .'

'Years . . . You *are* having problems with a case. What's it all about? Come on, let's go and sit down and you can get it off your chest. There's no hurry

172

to get the meal on. It's early.'

'No. I don't want to talk about it. I can't talk about it and I've told you, I'm tired of it all. If I got a proper job—'

'You? You mean leave the army? You?' She burst out laughing and gave him a hug. 'All right. I'll get the pasta on. You must be *really* hungry if it's as tragic as that. Go and have a shower.'

He held on to her.

'Go on! I can't cook with you in the way.'

He went.

*   *   *

In the afternoon it rained. No fussing and storming, apart from some low, distant thunder. Just steady rain. A soothing, regular patter. He leaned back against the soft coolness of leather and closed his eyes for twenty minutes or so in front of the television. He was aware of the newsreader's familiar voice and of Teresa moving about the flat, throwing back the shutters and opening the windows a little.

Once in a fresh uniform, ready to leave, he found her up a ladder with all the cupboards in the corridor open, pulling down parcelled-up winter woollies.

'Might as well take advantage of a day of without the boys—switch that light on for me, will you? I can't see what I'm doing.'

The rain-dark flat smelled of camphor.

He switched the light on and left.

He hadn't told her.

He'd have to tell the prosecutor, though, and it was impossible to guess whether he'd be relieved or alarmed. Or could he get away with not telling him? He thought about it, sitting at his desk, watching the rain fall outside his open window. In the three months of his notice, going his own way, could he solve . . . solve what? Apart from the fact that he couldn't, in any case, make a serious move without a warrant signed by the prosecutor, what could he possibly solve? His only real concern was to get those girls and, above all, the children, out of Paoletti's clutches. But what about the death of his daughter? In the end, it might well be Nesti who blew the whole Paoletti setup apart and uncovered the murderer in the process. At that point, the prosecutor would be forced to issue the necessary warrants. The press had more power than a marshal of carabinieri. Who did he think he was? A private investigator with excellent computer skills and a dynamic personality? That advert said it all.

So what was he going to say to the prosecutor? Probably nothing. Or rather, 'Yes, Mr. Prosecutor, no, Mr. Prosecutor,' like on the phone. If he could only stay in his office, talking to the people who came into the waiting room, where he belonged. The calm that had enveloped him while he was safe in his quarters, with Teresa moving quietly about, was leaving him, as the cold fat toad of anxiety squatting in his insides began to stir.

He got up and looked out at the waiting room. Nobody. Some wet footprints on the floor, a forgotten umbrella. He looked in at the duty room. The lads there were intent on their work and didn't even notice him. He couldn't put it off. And much as he would have preferred to be alone, he couldn't walk to the Procura in the rain either. He closed his window and summoned the youngest of his carabinieri to drive him. They got as far as the top of the staircase and stopped. The youngster snapped to attention and stood back. The marshal reopened the door and held it.

'Captain . . .'

Captain Maestrangelo reached the top of the staircase and came in without a word. His face was dark.

The two of them went into the marshal's office and sat down. They made no polite conversation. They were neither of them adept at it. Looking at him now, the marshal realized that Maestrangelo's face wasn't dark with anger, as sometimes happened, but with what seemed like pain. There were deep shadows under his eyes. Instead of reproaches, the marshal received only a request: 'If you wouldn't mind . . . a glass of water.'

The marshal stood up and went to get it himself.

The captain swallowed some pills, drank a little more of the water, and murmured: 'Bad headache. Politically sensitive cases are a headache in both senses . . .'

'The gypsy business . . . Of course. I'm sorry. I mean I'm sorry that, on top of that, I had to . . .'

'No.' The captain took the letter of resignation from the inside pocket of his jacket and placed it on the desk. 'No. Under no circumstances can I accept this. Whatever's wrong will be sorted out, but you're not going to resign.'

Not knowing at all what he should say, the marshal said nothing. The captain was a soft-spoken man, but today his voice was exceptionally low, as though the noise of it hurt his head.

'I know you have a family member sick, down at

175

home. If that's the problem, leave tomorrow. Go down to Syracuse, do what needs doing, and if you have to commute between here and there for a time, then do that. Be here to put your signature on the daily orders often enough so that I'm covered; and if the expense of the flights is a problem, I'll find a way to solve it.'

Still the marshal said nothing. He was both amazed and touched by what he'd heard, but it didn't change anything.

'That's not the problem, then?'

'No. No, that's not . . .'

'You must forgive me. I haven't had the time to follow much of this case you're on, but I saw in my morning's batch of cuttings that there's some scandal concerning this man, the victim's father.'

'Yes.'

'Your problem's with this case, then?'

The marshal planted his big hands on his knees and stared down at them.

'I am your superior officer.'

'Yes, sir.'

'But I can't order you to reveal anything covered by the secrecy of your investigation.'

'No, sir.'

'Guarnaccia . . .'

The marshal stared down at his hands. He listened to the rain.

'Is there no way at all for me to help you?'

'Yes, sir. I've written a report for the Procura of Genoa. Will you tell me whether I should address it to the Chief Public Prosecutor there—or is the Inspectorate . . . I've no experience in this sort of thing, and it's important that no time is wasted. It's very urgent.'

176

He raised his head now, wanting to transmit that urgency without any further explanation. They looked each other in the eyes for what seemed like a long time and he thought, *This is the only man in the world I really trust*. He almost weakened. The temptation to un- load this burden was almost too much for him. Almost, but not quite. He wasn't going to put Maestrangelo at risk. So he looked down at his hands again and waited.

The captain took out his pen and wrote on a sheet of paper which the marshal had passed across the desk.

'Given the urgency, you should transmit it. I'll have to make a phone call. Excuse me.' He called his own office for the e-mail address and wrote it underneath the name. The marshal took the sheet of paper from him.

'Thank you.' It was done.

Maestrangelo took another sip of water. He didn't get up to leave. He was frowning, and his eyes seemed dazed with pain.

The letter of resignation still lay there on the desk between them.

'I'm sorry, Guarnaccia. I really am. We both knew from the start that this prosecutor . . . I said you'd be all right and, though I've examined my conscience since receiving your letter, I really thought you would be all right. You've worked with him before . . .'

'Yes.'

'The first time, if I'm not mistaken, was in my absence.'

'You were away on holiday, yes.'

'Yes. And I might as well have been away on holiday this time, too, it seems.'

177

'No, no . . .'

'And then, I've always felt you were so much better at dealing with people than I could ever be—but these are not excuses. I've neglected you. I've let you down. And there's no excuse for that. My first duty of care is to you, not to the mayor. That you should come to this . . . without my even being aware that you were in difficulty—I'll tell you the truth, Guarnaccia: If there's one thing that grieves me more than the idea of losing you, it's losing your trust. That's just vanity, I suppose.'

'No. No, that's not right, not right at all. You haven't—no, no . . . it's what I have to do. It's better if the responsibility's mine, believe me.'

'I am your superior officer.'

'Yes, sir.'

'Taking responsibility is what I'm here for. The only reason for keeping this report of yours to yourself is that revealing its content to me would compromise your investigation. Would it?'

Why couldn't he leave it? Go back to his office, get on with his life, his career. He was too clever at talking.

'Would it compromise your investigation?'

'No.' It would compromise you, though. Don't insist. Please don't insist—but wasn't that what Piazza had said? Don't insist, Guarnaccia. And he had gone his own way because he was incapable of any other. *Your little independent ways . . . ,* as the prosecutor said.

'And yet you insist on taking it upon yourself to be the only one responsible. You're not. That's not how the army works. It may be how you work inside your own head; but have you thought about what happens if what you're trying to do goes

178

wrong? Are you sure you're capable of dealing with whatever this problem is, all alone? It's clearly something very serious indeed, or we wouldn't be having this conversation. I'm the last person to doubt your capabilities, Guarnaccia. I'm just saying think about the consequences—you know what they would be, I don't—if this report is inadequate in some way, if it doesn't communicate the urgency, the seriousness which I—knowing you and trusting you—believe in without question. Just remember that you're sending it to someone who doesn't know you and without my recommendation.'

The prosecutor had said the same thing, hadn't he? *You take too much upon yourself.*'

He hadn't thought, it was true. He'd done his best; but if his best wasn't good enough, if his best was an ill-written report—and he was no writer, any more than he was a talker—resulting in delays, even in a failure to convince at all? A florid man, balding, leaving the bedroom. A crying child. And all the weight of power and wealth against him.

The captain had picked up the letter of resignation and was holding it out. He took it and, in silence, gave him the report. The rain was coming down harder.

*   *   *

'Eternal rest give unto her, O Lord; and let perpetual light shine upon her . . .'

The church was very small but, even so, the marshal was puzzled by its being so full. His plan of sitting right at the back so as to watch everyone coming out was foiled since all the benches were

179

full. Nevertheless, he remained at the back on his feet and soon worked out that the greater part of the congregation was not in mourning and probably consisted of regular churchgoers here.

'We don't know anybody . . .' Hadn't the younger daughter said that one morning as they walked in the garden? Even some of those in black at the front of the church were a bit uncertain about kneeling and sitting, and the marshal felt sure that they were employees from Paoletti's club, under orders to dress for the occasion, who couldn't remember when they had last been at mass.

'I confess to Almighty God, to the Blessed Mary ever a Virgin, Blessed Michael the Archangel . . .'

If it came to that, he wasn't sure he could remember when he had last been at mass himself, so he was hardly the one to criticise.

'Through my fault, through my fault, through my most grievous fault . . .'

He'd been crazy to think he could take it upon himself . . . now he was following the captain's instructions to the letter.

'Just listen to whatever the prosecutor says and look compliant.'

He'd done that, silent, respectful, and, above all, expressionless.

'If he tells you to take some particular line of inquiry, as I imagine he has been doing until now . . .'

'Oh, yes. The daughter's private life, finding an ex-gardener who has a record, that sort of thing . . .' He was doing that, too. And since Paoletti, as expected, had to go back into hospital for tests, he was going to to follow the prosecutor's orders and stay close to the family. After all, they didn't want

something happening to the second daughter in his absence.

'He'll be out in a day or two.'

'And are you likely to be able to find this gardener?'

'I'll find him, just as slowly as the prosecutor wants. And to make it more convincing, we're doing a DNA check on the child. I'd thought . . . I'd hoped he might not want that, to be honest.'

'You didn't think De Vita could be—'

'No. Not him, no . . . I suppose I should have done. If he and Paoletti have been involved for years . . . and the murder occurred on his watch. That can hardly be luck, can it? No. You're right, I should have thought about it, but no. It's Paoletti I'm thinking of.'

'Incest?'

'Well, it's not a crime, strictly speaking, is it? Unless it's a public scandal or the child's under age. Paoletti likes respectability. He's ostentatious in his religion and his charitable donations. I know I'm not making myself clear, but everything in his life is controlled by him . . . He couldn't have killed her, it's true, and he wouldn't have wanted her killed by anybody else— even if she was trying to get away from him—not in his respectable household.'

'No. From what you've told me about him, I can quite see that. But that it happened on this particular prosecutor's watch is a consideration and, as you say, if you're right about the child's paternity, one would expect him to be reluctant to issue the warrant. Of course, he might not know.'

'And I might be wrong.'

'You might. In any case, the test will show if the child's parents are blood relations and besides, remember that what De Vita's trying to keep you away from may have nothing to do with your murder

181

case. It's probably only about saving his own skin.'

'Yes . . .'

'You're not convinced.'

He wasn't. But how could he explain that he felt the way those girls felt? That it made no difference whether Paoletti was in hospital when it happened or not: The hand of Paoletti was everywhere in this story. Whatever happened around Paoletti, he was guilty of it because he controlled everything. Poor Cristina had transmitted her fear to him, and he was finding it hard to shake off. Thinking she'd be on television. Would they be in time . . . ? Don Antonino would arrive this afternoon and be briefed.

The prosecutor would be suspended pending an investigation; but once he knew that, then Paoletti would be warned and the children would disappear. Everything had to be coordinated so that there was no time for Paoletti to act.

And even then, would they succeed in getting a conviction? There was the priest in the pulpit now, not talking about Daniela so much as about the heartfelt generosity of her father. Not only had he paid for the heating that had been installed in the church last autumn . . .

They must need it, too, the marshal thought, because it was ice-cold in here now, and it was still August.

He also intended, in the name of his dear daughter, so sadly taken from us, to restore the frescoes behind the altar . . .

Pink cherubs fluttering around a madonna in blue and white, hand to heart, eyes raised, soaring up to heaven on a damp-ravaged cloud with gold rays coming out of it.

All that pink and blue reminded the marshal of the bedroom ceiling in that hotel. Paoletti had no doubt restored that, too. The cold in here was yet another reminder of that long, unhappy night.

'Lord have mercy.

'Christ have mercy.

'Christ have mercy.

'Christ have mercy.

'Lord have mercy . . .'

All the money Paoletti had contributed to the church would explain why the congregation had turned out this morning, urged, no doubt, from the pulpit last Sunday.

How had they managed to get the mother up and dressed and to church at this hour? Of course, things must be different with Paoletti at home. However sick he might be, he would still be obeyed. They say some caged birds wouldn't fly away even though you left the cage door open. Paoletti knew how to choose his little birds. Fluttering captives.

'Eternal rest give unto her, O Lord . . .'

A child's whimper echoed. It must be Piero. He was silenced.

'And let perpetual light shine upon her . . .'

The marshal had this feeling about Paoletti: that, somehow, he would slip through their fingers. Even if the operation they were planning went perfectly, even though they had witnesses. After all, all those years ago, he'd been in a much tighter spot. He'd been arrested, there were witnesses, including his victim, and he hadn't the experience then that he did now—or a priest already on his side. How had he managed it that time? Thinking about Piazza and Paoletti's approach there, it occurred to him that the man had probably started out by having his confession heard and recruiting the priest that way. We all like to think we've saved somebody. Wasn't he guilty of that himself? Paoletti was such a clever manipulator. His antennae picked up people's weak spots and their little vanities too. And what about the sort of fancy lawyer his money would buy—no, he wouldn't even have to pay. That lawyer on his list of victims would do the job for free to protect himself. So clever . . . he would never go to prison, unless it was to leave right away by the back door like last time. The marshal admitted to himself that he was afraid of the man. Those children . . .

'Behold the Lamb of God, behold Him who taketh away the sins of the world . . .'

Communion was given at one side of the altar, since Daniela's coffin stood in the nave. Paoletti and his wife and daughter took communion before the rest of the congregation.

Just before the mass ended, the marshal retreated very quietly and stepped outside into the sun's heat, fishing for his dark glasses.

'I thought I'd find you here.'

'Nesti—you shouldn't be seen here, and especially not with me—'

'Let's go, then. Get in my car, I've got a surprise for you—and don't start! I've kept my word, haven't I?'

'Yes, but . . . who is that?'

'An important witness with something interesting to tell you about our friend Paoletti. Get in. They'll be coming out.'

'My own car and driver are here, and I have to go to the cemetery. What's this about?'

'Follow us, then. We'll go up to Trespiano and tuck our cars out of sight somewhere inside the cemetery gates. You can join the funeral when it arrives.'

Whoever the man in Nesti's car was, the marshal didn't recognize him, but he followed them down through the city and up the via Bolognese. The steep, narrow road was strewn with purple ribbons and lost flower heads blown from speeding hearses.

Inside the cemetery, the marshal and the stranger stood in the strip of shade offered by a line of cypresses while Nesti walked up and down, smoking, keeping an eye out for the arrival of the Paoletti cortège.

The stranger introduced himself as an ex-colleague with the same grade as the marshal.

'I saw that piece in the paper and so I rang up. Nesti said I should talk to you.'

'You know something about this murder?'

'Murder? No. But I know something about Paoletti. I was marshal out there up to a couple of years ago, before Piazza.'

'You . . . you look young to have retired . . .'

'Retired? Well, I suppose you could say retired. I took on Paoletti and lost—not deliberately, I'm no hero. I heard rumours about that hotel and decided to do a bit of nighttime investigating. Saw people I shouldn't have seen. Anyway, I found myself transferred.'

'Where?'

'Basilicata. I've nothing against the south, but my wife's from Bologna . . . you know how it is. Anyway, to cut a long story short, they didn't come with me, they went to her mother's—just at first,

185

the wife said, and then . . . After a while I realized they'd never come. Kids liked their schools there, and so on. So, I took early retirement.'

'Could you afford it? I mean . . .'

'Of course I couldn't afford it. Could you?'

'No. No, I . . .'

'Watch your back, then. He's dangerous and he's well-connected.'

'I know. Lucky for me, my commanding officer—'

'A company captain? Don't kid yourself. You'll both be out on your ear. Don't mess around with him. You'll be the one to lose out. There are politicians involved. You follow me?'

'Is that all you came to tell me?'

'No, it's not, but it's one of the things, so if you've got a family . . .'

'What . . . what did you do? I mean, after you left the army?'

'Moved in with her mother. What else could I do?'

'And . . .' He wanted to ask if it had turned out all right, but he could see that it hadn't. Everything about the man showed that he no longer had a wife. The day was very hot, of course, but that was yesterday's shirt giving off the smell of stale sweat and his hair was just a bit too long and smelled of . . . hair. The marshal changed his question. 'Did you find work?'

'Eventually. Security job. Boring. Didn't get on too well with the mother-in-law, though, so . . . You know how it is.'

'You said that you had something else to tell me.'

'I've got plenty to tell you if you're sure you want to keep after him.'

'I'm sure.'

186

'Well then—Wait—it looks like they're here.'

Nesti was signalling the arrival of the funeral procession. There was nothing for it but to interrupt. The marshal's presence there was official, furthering the pretence of looking for the unknown father of little Piero. The other two men must not be seen, so they arranged to meet at the same spot when it was all over.

The marshal got into his car. Only three cars followed the hearse apart from his own, one with the family, the other two with employees. At the burial niche, the marshal recognized Frida and Danuta. The others he wasn't so sure about, but, judging by their size and aspect, at least two of them he reckoned were bouncers from the club and a young thin one could well be the character in the orange baseball cap. Was he perhaps the Mauro who drove the two cleaning girls back and forth between the villa here and the club and Cristina and the rest between the club and the hotel? It was only a guess, of course, but the marshal, staring at the back of his head, bare today, felt sure of it and sure, too, that he acted as postman. Something was wrong, though . . . to do with his driving the girls . . .

He couldn't see the priest, a short man, beyond the broad backs of the bouncers, but he heard the quiet clink of the aspergillum as he blessed the coffin.

'May her soul and the souls of all the faithful departed, through the mercy of God, rest in peace.'

'Amen.'

Above them, the rainwashed cypresses raised sharp black sihouettes to the clean blue sky.

Teresa would be there by now. He'd put her on the seven twenty flight to Catania.

'I'll get a taxi straight to the hospital.'

'I'm sorry . . . I mean—'

'It doesn't matter—I understand how you feel about the two children—but you shouldn't take things so personally. It's still only a case.'

'Yes . . .' He couldn't tell her the truth.

What was it he was trying to remember about the driver? It would come back to him. The brief word with his ex-colleague had agitated him. You can't remember things if you're agitated. You can't observe things properly, either. Of all those standing around the coffin on its trestles, it was the mother he would have liked to observe, but he couldn't see her face. There was a brief moment, when the group moved to allow the coffin to be slid into its niche in the wall, when he got a good look at Paoletti. He looked distressed. His face was paler and looked collapsed. After all, he was just a man who'd lost his first-born child. Frida and Danuta were standing to one side, a little apart, and he had a good view of them. They had little Piero between them. They each held one of his hands, and he kept trying to swing on them. The girls were dressed in black, but their short dresses and high heels looked more suitable for waiting on customers in the club than for a funeral, and so did their makeup. All that black eye makeup made the pale little things look haggard in the sunlight.

As for the mother, when he did manoeuvre himself into a position where he could see her, the marshal was surprised. On this day, of all days, she could have been expected to have an incapacitating hangover. But she was sober, well-

188

groomed, and calm. Her face was expressionless. Moving again, he saw Silvana in profile, crying, leaning against her father. He put an arm around her, murmuring something that quietened her when her crying became audible. She put on a pair of dark glasses and stood up straight. But then she was obedient. The marshal himself had found her so. Surely, though, even Paoletti's authority couldn't cure an alcoholic overnight . . .

'She doesn't drink!'

Silvana had snapped at him that first morning when he'd suggested she give her mother a drop of something to revive her. It would have worked, too. She had been too hungover—or even still too drunk—to register her daughter's death. Of course, it was possible that she had been taking advantage of her husband's absence to drink so much, but the timetable of the two girls who came and got her up at midday . . .

'Don't hold on to the table. Lean on me.' They were used to dealing with it.

'My mother's not well . . .'

All that stuff didn't square with her composure this morning. Yet he was a witness to both states.

What *was* it he needed to remember about the driver, Mauro? The group standing before the niche was breaking up. The builders began walling it up. The low sun burned strong and clean this morning, so that the red icon lights on the marble plaques of the other niches burned in reflection. All the little bunches of flowers, real or plastic, still held unshed raindrops. He wanted to talk to the mother, the way she was now, sober. But Nesti and his ex-colleague were waiting for him, and he had no choice but to watch the cars drive away and

189

then join them near the gates. Daniela was dead, buried now, and he had to give priority to those who were still in danger. He was going to have to be careful, too, since he shouldn't tell the man anything he didn't already know. It was obvious from his first question that he knew nothing about Daniela's death.

'So, who were they burying?'

'Paoletti's daughter, Daniela.'

'His daughter? You mentioned a murder before—you don't mean that she—'

'Yes. You didn't see that in the paper?'

'No—well, I confess I wasn't taking much notice. Just saw Paoletti's name and thought "Right, that's it." I'm out of the army now and I can say what I want, you know what I mean? He's probably trodden on somebody's toes if they've gone for the daughter. I can't be any help to you on that. It's Paoletti himself I'm concerned with, him and De Vita.'

'De Vita? Fulvio De Vita?'

'The prosecutor.'

'You've seen Paoletti's list, then?'

'I haven't seen any list. I suppose there had to be one. A list of the people who could be blackmailed—if that's what you mean.'

The marshal glanced about him. Nesti was standing at a distance. He knew how to go after stuff, but he knew how to be discreet and wait too.

'Yes, that's what I mean. De Vita's one of the people on it, so—'

'De Vita's on it, is he? You've got to hand it to that bastard Paoletti, he's always one step ahead. Well, why not? With photographs, no doubt. I never saw any, but I know they took photographs.

So De Vita's on this list, eh? A sort of insurance policy in case he ever wanted to get out.'

'Get out . . .'

'You're not there yet, are you? Prosecutor De Vita may be on that list as an insurance policy, but he and Paoletti are in this together. They've been a double act for years. That's what I found out by accident, and that's what cost me my job.'

Ten

'Yes, Your Excellency, exactly. No, that all remains in place, but I'll need to talk to this ex-marshal and then perhaps send him to you. The better informed we are are, the fewer risks . . . tomorrow, rather than today. Guarnaccia informs me that Paoletti has checked into the hospital for twenty-four hours for blood tests, and it's essential we bring them all in together . . . yes. Yes. I don't think he'll get away from us this time even so, Your Excellency. Ah. That's very good news. That will make all the difference. I'll tell him immediately and yes, at three here. Good morning, Your Excellency.'

The marshal waited. From what he'd heard, it sounded like good news, but he was anxious to hear the Chief Public Prosecutor's half of the conversation.

Captain Maestrangelo reassured him at once.

'I know what you want to hear first. The new prosecutor is the one you hoped for.'

'Good, good—he used to be a children's judge and I'm sure he'll follow up the question of these two afterwards. He still has the contacts, you see, and, besides, he's a good man. I mean, it's the children he'll care about, not the television cameras.'

'And you can tread water on the Paoletti murder for another day or so without arousing suspicion?'

'Yes. I'm following up the ex-gardener, Marco Melis. It may take me a day or two to establish without any doubt—and produce the documentation to prove—what I already know about him from a couple of telephone calls.'

'Which is?'

'That he's inside, has been for fifteen months.'

'But the prosecutor will surely realize how quickly you could have found that out.'

'No. Paoletti only gave me his name, no place or date of birth.'

'So how did the database bring him up? It must be the most common name in Sardinia.'

'Yes. But Paoletti's only been inside once. I thought that would be where they met. There's a record of Paoletti's arrest in the station where it was made, and he was remanded in Sollicciano. There was a Marco Melis there at the time. It was a roundabout sort of business finding out, and I had to use some personal contacts, so . . . And then, he . . .'

'What?'

'Well, I've worked with this man before, as you remember. He knows I'm a bit slow.'

Captain Maestrangelo smiled. A fleeting smile, but a smile nevertheless.

'And so this Melis is of no use in your inquiry beyond an excuse to tread water?'

'I shouldn't think so. He's Paoletti's age, for a

192

start. I'd been thinking of a handsome young lad and those two daughters so confined. No, no . . . And still there's one thing about him that does interest me and, if there's ever time, I'd like to talk to him about it later.'

'What's that?'

'He got away from Paoletti, something not even our prosecutor can do.'

'The Sardinian character. Might break but won't bend.'

'That's true.'

*   *   *

The marshal waited. He and the captain together had talked to Don Antonino, and he was ready for the arrival of the women. The organization of tomorrow's coordinated raids on Paoletti's villa, club, and hotel was in someone else's hands, and he didn't think about it. Even so, his awareness of all that activity going on out of sight left him free to be still and quiet at the centre. He watched and listened, sometimes in his own office, taking calls, sometimes in the carabinieri car parked inside the villa's gates, sometimes in the oppressive kitchen, watching Danuta and Frida go up and down the stairs, wearing rubber gloves and carrying brushes and plastic buckets. The stiller and quieter he was, the more things were revealed to him, both big and small. Impressions, details, images. He didn't grasp at them, only recorded them in his head.

He noticed, for instance, that Danuta, who had at first seemed indistinguishable from Frida in that they were both young, thin, and colourless, had a slight squint in one eye, a defect that had surely

193

saved her from the second floor of the hotel. Once he'd noticed that, he watched Frida, who must also have some defect. He soon found it out. Under her thin, cheap T-shirt, he could see that she had hardly any breasts. That was on the evening of the day of the funeral. He had been there all afternoon, walking around the grounds, watching from a distance as Silvana and Frida played with the little boy in the pool, sitting out in his car and saying a few words to his driver, returning to the crime scene up in the tower, walking around the grounds again, circling closer and, as it started getting dark, coming inside. He asked no questions of anybody; he just wanted to be there. There was no sign of the mother. He supposed she knew he was there and was in her bedroom up on the first floor. Silvana was up there, too, somewhere. He'd heard her earlier playing the piano. Every now and then she sang a few notes, quiet, hesitant, and then stopping. It had seemed out of place to the marshal, music on the afternoon of the funeral, but he'd been the one to suggest it, he recalled, and anything was better than her crying. Judging by the dishes on the table, the evening meal was over. Frida had already put the little boy to bed. They had improvised a bedroom for him and Frida on the ground floor, and the marshal himself had brought over the long-nosed fluffy animal from his bed in the tower.

It was almost nine. Both girls were in the kitchen, clearing up. Perhaps because her Italian was better than Frida's, it was Danuta who, when they'd finished, dared to say, 'We eat something at this time. I have to go . . .'

'That's all right. Eat.'

They ate at a marble worktop near the fridge, sitting on high stools, silent. Aware that his presence embarrassed them, he got up and climbed the stairs to go out to his two men in the parked car inside the gates of the villa.

It was dark.

He got into his own car which, hours earlier, his driver had taken care to park in the shade. The front passenger seat was pleasantly cool, but the driver was more than a little heated. The marshal appreciated his energy and enthusiasm and would have been only too pleased to satisfy his curiosity, but what was there to tell him? That his own memory was failing him? That he couldn't for the life of him work out what didn't add up about those girls, only that it had something to do with this moment? The child was in bed. Frida was kept here because Silvana couldn't be left to cope alone—well, not to be unreasonable, the child wasn't hers and there was a drunken mother in the mix—so be it . . .

Mauro, the driver, postman, setter-up of compromising photographs . . . had it something to do with him?

'Marshal . . . ?'

'I won't be a minute.' He got out and went over to the other car. One of the two carabinieri was talking quietly into the radio. The window was wound down. The driver turned the ignition.

'No, no . . . nothing yet. I wanted to ask you something. Were either of you two on duty here last Saturday night?'

'Not me,' the driver said. 'Only got back from my holidays on Sunday—you were, weren't you?'

'The night you came, late on, to ask how it was

195

going? Yes, I was here. You didn't talk to me, though, I remember. It was my partner—'

'Who said two young women left in the black mini.'

'Yes. That was what you—'

'And he said they had tits on them like . . . I don't know what. Is that right?'

'You know what it's like . . . I mean, sitting here for hours. He didn't mean anything by it.'

'Right.'

'What's the matter with him . . . ?'

The marshal overheard that, but he didn't stop to explain. He went back to his own car.

'Is something happening?' The young carabiniere reached for the ignition.

'No, no. Don't.'

He got into the car and sat still a moment, trying to decide what was best. Mauro hadn't been seen here, and neither of those two girls would have driving licences. What should he do? The driver beside him was young, inexperienced. To send the other two would be better, but if something happened here? The marshal himself had to stay in the house, which would leave this boy out here alone. No . . .

Should he call for backup? On what grounds? A vulgar remark? No. He must decide.

You take it upon yourself . . .

Your little independent ways . . .

He tried these remarks on himself a few times, to no effect. Water off a duck's back. Inside, he was calm.

'You're going to have to do something for me—no. No, don't turn your engine on yet. Two women will come out and drive away in the mini—'

'You want me to follow them?'

'Yes . . . and no. I can't leave here, but I need to know who drives the car. That's all.'

'You don't want to know where it goes?'

'I don't know . . . They'll probably take the motorway and go out to Paoletti's club. If that's the road they take, just come back.'

'Oh . . . right.' He sounded disappointed. 'There's no radio in here, though . . .'

'Keep your distance from the mini, turn back if they take the motorway. Don't be in a hurry to follow them. There's hardly any traffic, and I'd rather they didn't notice you if you can manage that. Call me on your mobile if there's anything. That's all.'

He went back down to the kitchen, empty now, and waited, listening. Before too long, he heard footsteps above; the door. The car doors. The engine. Then it was quiet.

He was sitting at the table where he had sat on his first morning here, running over images from that day. The still water of the pool, the sunlight on the rumpled white bed, that fine spray of blood on the side, shattered glass . . .

He ran the whole morning again, knowing now about the prosecutor. But what did he really know about him? That it had happened on his watch, very conveniently on his watch.

In his new subdued, compliant role, the marshal had demonstrated to De Vita his total concentration on matters other than The Emperor yesterday by talking about the ex-gardener, hoping to elicit two more warrants besides the one for the child's DNA. One for a search of this whole house, in case a weapon was missing that Paoletti hadn't noticed. That was refused.

'*I can see no necessity for it. What makes you think he has any weapons?*' the prosecutor had asked.

'*Just the fact that one was used, and not a professional's weapon, as we agreed at the time. There was no one in the house except Paoletti's wife. She was asleep and she wears earplugs . . . Anyone could have got in.*'

'*I think all that's necessary is that I ask him myself once the funeral's over. I can see no need to disturb the family.*'

Weapons. He had said 'weapons,' not 'a weapon.' Well, that had been refused.

The other warrant he would have liked was one to pull the phone records for the whole household; but, needless to say, that hadn't materialized, only one for the victim's number.

'*That's already in hand. Now, I want you to stay close to the family until Paoletti has had these tests done in the hospital and is back at home. I understand they're monitoring his blood pressure for twenty-four hours. We don't want anything untoward happening in his absence. Imagine how that would look.*'

Well, it was all nonsense, of course, but, even so, the phrases he used . . . Anything untoward . . . how it would look . . .

'Hmph . . .' He stood up. He was here to 'stay close to the family.' So, where were they? He had so far been excluded from anywhere except the entrance and this kitchen; but now he was going to stay close, as instructed. He started up the stairs with a sensation that he remembered from childhood: the excitement of that very rare occurrence, being alone in the house. Why a house looks so different to a child left alone is a mystery. Every room takes on a personality, forbidding, secretive, with its own special smell, and an opened drawer provokes tingles of guilty excitement. He remembered once, he was walking with his mother along the pale, dusty lane to the village to shop, and she had sent him back because she'd forgotten her list. Why were they walking there? They had their first Fiat 500 then, surely. Maybe his father was already in the village and was going to drive them back with the shopping. It was a long walk.

He'd found the list right away on the kitchen table, but he'd lingered. It was early on a summer morning, and his mother had already baked a sponge ring and cooked some green beans. Both were cooling on the kitchen table. It would be too hot to cook anything but the pasta and a thin slice of meat later. The beans didn't interest him but, of course, the cake did. He'd managed to slide one finger under it and withdraw a morsel. It was warm and buttery and so much better than it would be later, a cold slice on a plate. He'd confessed it on the Saturday. Wickedness in a silent house.

Up on the ground floor, he stood and listened. To his right, the door to the library was closed. He knocked, waited, opened it, and switched the lights on. Glimpsed through the door the other day, the high room had been impressive, but from inside he could see into the wings of what was a bit of a stage set. Those wall-to-ceiling shelves facing the door were filled with matching leather-bound volumes, Boccaccio, Tasso, Ariosto, Dante. They were new but a little dusty and quite probably unopened. Paoletti's big, ornate desk where he'd been sitting the other day was used. The stuff on it was mostly household bills and bank statements, but there was a biggish photograph in a silver frame. He picked it up. Paoletti and a thin, dark-haired child. That must be Silvana. She looked about six or seven. He was bending down towards her as though telling her something special, and she was gazing up at him, head tipped to one side, a winning smile, a strand of long hair twined around her finger. They were totally absorbed in one another. He put it down. The shutters of the three tall French windows were closed. There were huge expensive-looking carpets. When he turned to leave, though, he saw that the shelves flanking the doors were empty, though there were a couple of cardboard boxes there with more books wrapped in transparent packaging. There was a white formica table in the corner loaded with electronic stuff, with a tangle of black wires and white cables underneath. There were more boxes, too. Big ones, closed with shiny brown packaging tape, their contents scribbled with a black felt-tip. 'Office stationery,' 'spare light fittings,' 'summer shoes.' That suggested that they'd been there since the family had moved into the house. The condition of Paoletti's wife would explain that.

He switched off the light as he left and crossed the hall. Again, he knocked, waited, and then went in. This was a very big room, twice the size of the other, with a dining room and sitting room divided from each other by an arch. Six tall shuttered windows, more expensive carpets, a gigantic vase of artificial flowers. But there were three cardboard boxes in here, too.

A respectable old age under construction. A long

200

way from running prostitutes down at the park.

As was always the case, the one person he needed to talk to was dead. Daniela Paoletti somehow seemed separate from all this pretension. Her rooms were simple and appropriately furnished, her books read. Would she have got away from here once she finished her studies? The lodger, her mother called her.

He left the room and walked back past the iron railing of the kitchen staircase. Further along was another staircase up to the next floor, and beyond that a cloakroom and the improvised child's bedroom. His footsteps on the stone floor were loud in the dead silence. Water flushed and the cloakroom door opened. Frida came out, barefoot and wearing a long T-shirt.

'Everything all right?'

She nodded.

'The little boy asleep?'

Another nod. He wasn't sure she'd even understood him.

'Frida!' Piero came running out in his vest, trailing his fluffy toy by the nose. He stopped dead when he saw the marshal.

'Shouldn't you be in bed? It's very late.'

'I have to wait for Frida. Look.' He held up the toy. 'Do you know his name now?'

'Oh . . . oh dear, I've forgotten.'

'It's Nosey!'

'Nosey, that's right.'

'Don't forget again!'

'I won't. And you be good, for Frida.'

'She's my mummy now.'

'Good night.'

He watched them go in and shut the door. His

phone rang.

'Marshal?'

'Where are you?'

'Piazzale Michelangelo.'

'What?'

'I followed the car—I don't think she's seen me. They went to the station first and the blonde girl got out there and went in, so I suppose she caught a train. I carried on following the car. Should I have followed the blonde one? Only, you said . . .'

'No, no. You did right. And she drove up there? What's she doing now?'

'I'm not sure. She stopped the car and went in that little bar. Then she walked to the balustrade and looked down at the city like everybody else. The place is crawling with tourists, so I'm parked where I can see her car. I thought if I got out, I might lose her in the crowd . . . wait a minute. I can see her again. She's still near the balustrade, chatting up some American students. They're trying to get her to drink from a wine bottle. It looks to me like they're laughing at her. What do you want me to do?'

'Nothing. Tell me how she's dressed.'

'It's pretty dark. Those big white globe things don't really give that much light.'

'But you saw her up here when she got in the car. I know it was dark then, too, but give me an idea. Was her skirt long or short?'

'Oh, I can tell you that. Short, really short. I mean, getting into a mini . . . and a low-cut top. I noticed that. What should I do next?'

'Wait and follow her home.'

'What if she goes off with somebody? It looks like that's what she's after.'

'If she does, ring me. But I don't think she will.'

Even when the cage is open . . .

He went back down to the kitchen and got himself a glass of water. That first morning, sitting where he sat now, he had watched her cry, squeezing sodden tissues that showed a trace of eye makeup. She was twenty-odd years old and her idea of rebellion was to throw off her daddy's little-girl persona and go up to the piazzale in short skirt and makeup to flirt. He really didn't believe she did more than flirt, or she'd have been gone from here long ago. And she drove Danuta to the train. So nobody belonging to the club was seen around here after the murder. No doubt Mauro would pick Danuta up at the other end. One little mystery solved, for what it was worth. He waited, alert for the sound of her car, wondering what it must be like to have daughters to worry about. He knew some of his colleagues had their daughters followed. It was all wrong, in his opinion, but seeing the things they saw, it was difficult to blame them. When it came to Paoletti, women were his property, to be bought and sold, put to to work, controlled. It was easy enough to see why he would marry a prostitute, even without his need to stop her testifying against him. But his own daughter? She was his property too, and even more dependent than the girls who worked for him. Even so . . .

There. That was the car. A father would go to the door and say 'What time do you call this?' But it wasn't yet eleven, and she was a grown woman. He heard the door, her footsteps on the stairs going up to her room. A tiny, rather pathetic rebellion against the ruler. Daniela, perhaps, was a more serious case, his as a daughter, his as a wife. The marshal was quite sure of that. He couldn't allow her to break free, and he had a prosecutor at his service and an alibi. He could hardly have predicted his stroke, though. Whatever had gone wrong, it had to have started there.

His phone rang.

'Is that you? Yes, she's come in. You did well.'

'Are we staying here all night?'

'I don't know. Are you tired?'

'No!'

Anything but tired. He was evidently pleased. Well, it's an ill wind . . .

Another small mystery he could solve was to find out what was in what he thought of as the servants' quarters down here, other than a broom cupboard and storage space where the cleaners kept their stuff. Somebody had been watching him the other morning from there, whatever Silvana said about the girls not arriving until twelve. He had no search warrant, but—though he couldn't risk going up to the first-floor bedrooms, disturbing the family members, possibly provoking a call to the prosecutor—he was going to take a look in there if it wasn't locked.

He got up and walked across to the closed door. As with the other rooms, he went through the formality of knocking before grasping the handle.

'What do you want?'

He was too shocked to reply for a moment, though he recognized the voice.

'You can come in.'

He opened the door. He thought of 'I'm sorry to disturb you,' or 'I just want to know you're all right.' But he only stood in the doorway and took the scene in. High, barred windows like in the kitchen, a big room, a white bed. The woman was sitting in an armchair next to it, alone in the silence.

'It's not what you think,' she said.

'Signora . . .'

'Come in.'

He went through an anteroom with metal broom cupboards on each side and entered the big room. She was in her nightdress. She was sweating. He could smell that and the drink. She wasn't quite drunk, though, because she had a book in her lap.

'No, this is not a prison, Marshal. That's what you're thinking, so don't say you're not. This whole building . . .' She looked up at the high, horizontal windows with their thick curved grills. 'It looks like a prison, but it was built to keep people out, not in. That's true of my bit of it, too. I don't do the stairs, you see. It would interfere with my drinking. So I stay here. You might as well sit down.'

He looked about him, hesitating.

'It will have to be on the bed. This is the only chair. I don't have visitors. I can give you a drink, though. Whisky?'

'No, no . . . thank you.' He sat on the edge of the bed near its foot, where there was a big television. It was on but without the sound.

She saw him glance at it before turning to her. 'There's never anything worth watching. It's the colour and movement. It keeps me company, like a fire might. I suppose that sounds ridiculous.'

'No . . . I've done the same myself.'

'You?'

'I've been alone a lot lately.'

She picked up the bottle. 'You're sure you . . . ?'

'No.'

'You don't drink? Well, if you don't need it.' She put the bottle down on the bedside table between her chair and the bed and stroked it. 'My best friend and adviser. I suppose you think I'm an alcoholic.'

'No.'

'Of course. You were at the funeral.'

'Yes.'

'Well, some people can put on a show of being sober.'

The marshal said nothing.

'But you're not the sort to be convinced by a show.'

'No.'

She drank. Her glass was a tumbler and it was over half full. She put it down and closed the book on her knees.

'Not even the wonderful show put on by my husband, I suppose. I drink too much. Even when I don't really want to, I still drink too much. It anaesthetises me for the evening and knocks me out so that I sleep for a long, long time.'

'And when you wake up?'

'I have a hangover, if that's what you mean, and that's the most important thing. Getting the hangover just right. It's not a question of how much I can drink without making a fool of myself. I sit here on my own and then fall into bed. It's the hangover that counts. The thing is to get through the afternoon in a fog, still a bit drunk and with just enough of a headache. It's like a glass wall, keeping all their voices out. Too much makes me sick and the headache's too painful, too little lets the voices through.'

206

'And the earplugs keep the voices out, too?'

'That's after supper. I get through the family meal he insists on, and then I escape and shut myself in here. The earplugs keep his voice out. He shouts.'

Instinct told him he could trust this woman, but caution warned him that he couldn't rely on an alcoholic. She was also frightened of her husband. She never said his name. There was a telephone by her bed. One call from the hospital, checking up on her, would be enough. There was so much she could tell him, but at this eleventh hour he daren't risk the children's lives. He must only speak to her as though the prosecutor himself were in the room.

'If I'm not mistaken, the first time I saw you, you had more than just enough of a headache.'

'You mean the day . . . . they got me up. I can't be got up.'

'No. I can understand that—and I didn't mean to disturb you now. I was checking through the building. It's just a precaution. Your daughter's safely home and has gone up to bed.'

'Where's Piero?'

'In bed. Frida's with him. And I have two cars and three men just outside.'

'Well, that's all right, then.' Her ironic glance spoke volumes. 'He won't like it, you know, your discovering me in here.'

'I'm sorry. I was just checking round the house. I had no idea, otherwise . . .'

He looked about him. The bed he was sitting on was big and its counterpane snowy white. It reminded him of Daniela's room in the tower. Everything here was clean and simple. The door at the far side of the room no doubt led to a bathroom and he imagined that, too, being like Daniela's. Dark blue and white. Clean and simple again—even if the cleanliness here was thanks to Frida and Danuta. Mother and daughter looked alike. Blonde, plump, and pink. Paoletti had replaced his wife with the younger, fresher version. All in the family, all under control. And if she had been underage when it started, no one could prove that now. He was too clever. He was always operating just inside the law, always in control. And yet something had got out of control . . . a messy murder in his respectable house. He couldn't have wanted it. Something had got out of his control when he was in hospital, and whatever it was . . . he was sure it must have started with the stroke.

They'd never get him. Somebody else would get the blame for Daniela and for all the rest. Everything on paper would be in order, he was always somewhere else, and this morning's priest would be his character witness.

'Are you going to arrest my husband?' She was looking at him, apparently reading his mind.

'I . . . it's not really for me to decide what—'

'Of course not. That would be Fulvio's decision. Fulvio was once a regular . . . customer . . . of mine. Had strange tastes. Preferred watching to anything. He's my husband's lapdog, as I'm sure you've noticed. I think he's frightened of him.'

He had to change the subject, steer her away from this dangerous ground.

'You're from the north, I remember. Do you still have family there?'

'Family? I've no idea. Families . . .' She made a

208

little spitting sound of disgust. 'I worked for a family up there before I ran away. My father chucked me out at sixteen because his new wife didn't like me, and I went as a nanny, unqualified, paid a pittance. A very respectable family. Husband was screwing me, wife threw me out. Usual thing.'

'Why did you choose Florence?'

'Florence . . . ?'

Did she even remember or care, shut up in here, that Florence was where she lived?

'I went to Milan. There was this boy, Daniele, the one I ran away with. When the money ran out, he said he had contacts here and I should follow him. When I didn't hear, I hitched a lift . . .'

'Did you ever find him?'

'Of course not. I don't suppose he ever left Milan. He'd dumped me, that's all. I really liked him—I still think about him sometimes. I don't blame him. We were so young, and I'd have done the same in his place. You sure you won't . . . ?'

'No.'

'You're working, I suppose. Pardon me if I do.' She filled her glass. 'Don't worry, I don't get maudlin. I just wonder sometimes where he is, that's all. Daniele . . . let's hope he did better than me. Just look at me.'

'Do you never go out? At least into the garden?'

'Garden? I used to, when the children were young. Not now. Not here.'

'You do go out, though. Your neighbour, Signora Donati across the road, mentioned that she sees you all going off to church on Sunday mornings.'

'That's *him*—and I don't know any Signora Donati.'

'No, she didn't say she knew you—it's just that her garden overlooks your gates, so . . . I don't really know her myself, but her son did his military service with us, so we got talking . . .' He caught that ironic glance again and corrected himself. 'I'm sorry. I had to question her because of your daughter's death. I thought she might have seen somebody leaving here that morning.'

'And did she?'

'No.'

'I suppose I can't testify against him even now, can I?'

'No.'

'No . . . but there are more ways than one of— I'm getting a bit too drunk for this conversation, but you've got to understand: Everything that happens in this house is down to him, and if my daughter's dead, it's due to him, hospital or no hospital. I can't testify, but I can help you, even so. He's taken one daughter from me . . .' She touched a photograph in a silver frame standing behind the whisky bottle. 'How thin she was, poor thing. It's hard to believe it now, but I was happy that year— or at least as near to happy as I ever got.'

'The year of her First Communion. She was happy then, too, maybe. She had that same photograph by her bed.' He remembered it with a bullet hole, the bullet embedded in the carving of the bedside cabinet. 'She is very thin. How old is she there?'

'Ten. And I thought we could play happy families. He just wanted more people he could order about—you've got to arrest him. It's all his fault! I know I'm drunk, but I'm telling you the truth. Whatever happened, it's his fault.'

210

He wanted to say Yes. Yes, I believe you. He didn't dare. He said nothing.

'Have to go to bed.'

He stood up and held out his arm to help her.

'No. I don't need . . .' With a sideways movement she sat down heavily on the bed.

'I'll come and see you tomorrow.'

'He's coming home tomorrow. Come in the afternoon. He'll be out. I heard him on the phone . . .'

'The afternoon, then. It could be . . .' Could he risk it? He stuck to the script, at least, ' . . . that you or your husband will be asked whether there are any guns in the house. The prosecutor didn't want to disturb you by—'

'Fulvio? If there are any guns! Like he doesn't know there's a collection of them. He's here every other night. *He* used to drag us all to the shooting range with him. Showing off what a brilliant shot he was. And Fulvio was there, too, more often than not. If there are any guns in the house . . .'

She was reaching for the earplugs by her bed. He could only hope that he could take her word for it, that drunkenness, sleep, hangover, and the earplugs would protect her—and Paoletti's other prisoners—until tomorrow. He left her.

He felt he shouldn't go home. The game he was playing with the prosecutor had to be kept up. Even so, he couldn't stand one more minute of this kitchen. He tried his best, walking around the huge room, looking at all the stuff. It was like the kitchen of a big restaurant with every kind of professional-looking equipment. Why would you need that great big bacon slicer? All that expanse of marble, lit by dozens of neon strips? Was it like the books upstairs? Had Paoletti ordered a kitchen wholesale that wouldn't be put to good use any more than the books would ever be read? Round and round he walked, but it was no use. He couldn't stay down there. He gave up on it, climbed the stairs and went along the flagged passageway to open the front doors. He walked across the gravel to the cars. He could hear the radio coughing into life and going off.

'All right?'

'Quiet as the grave. That's us! Thank God, I'm starving.'

Another car was nosing in. The next shift.

The marshal's driver was out of the car, walking up and down.

'I just needed to stretch my legs.' He got back in the car and the marshal got in beside him.

'Are we leaving?'

'No. I'm just going to keep you company for a while. Everybody inside is asleep.'

'What's going to happen next?'

'Nothing.'

He said that more to reassure himself than anything. He'd left one of the outside lights on over the front doors. He'd have left all of them on, but the rest were on automatic timers and would only go off again. He had the keys in his pocket. Both cars had a view of the big studded doors. The ones at the other end of the flagged passageway that gave onto the gardens were locked and bolted on the inside with great iron bars. The two family cars were parked to the right of the marshal's, under the trees.

Not to keep people in but to keep people out, she said. Prying people. People like him who

212

wanted to uncover the family secrets. It occurred to him that Paoletti might be aiming to make enough money to sell the club, the hotel, all of it, and distance himself from the source of his wealth. That might explain his carving up of this place. To cut himself off from his past, he needed money, a lot of it. He was on the verge of starting his new life, ready for his role as a restorer of churches, a pillar of the community, a respectable old age. The unread books were on the shelves on one side of the library, but on the other they were still in their boxes. He'd been interrupted. He'd lost control. The stroke . . .

The marshal opened the car door.

'What is it?'

'Nothing. I just want to take a look around. You stay here.'

He wanted to go back to the start. Even in the dark, he wanted to stand by the pool as he had on that morning. It might help him to see everything in the new light of Prosecutor De Vita's involvement. He turned the corner of the tower and went round to the far side of the swimming pool to stand there. The city lay below him, its palaces illuminated. Long glittering chains showed where the River Arno snaked between the buildings. The moon was bright enough, now all that rain had washed the air. The grass under his feet was springy and wet. He turned and stepped onto the tiled border to keep his feet dry. He looked up at the tower's silhouette in the moonlight. Had 'the lodger' been locked in up there, or had she tried to lock her family out? Didn't it, in the end, come to the same thing? Whatever family had built this place and shut out

213

the war or the plague, they'd been shut in too, hadn't they?

Besides, you could try and shut the plague out, but cancer . . . stroke, too. He kept coming back to it. It had to have started then.

What's going to happen next? Nothing, or . . .

He was as sure as the mother in her drunken stupor underground that whatever had happened was Paoletti's fault, and still it had happened in his absence.

Plague, cancer, stroke, people locked in and people locked out . . .

No point in breaking his head over it. Once the raids were over, the arrests made, the mother would talk. Despite everything she said, she was vigilant. She was intelligent, too, like her dead daughter.

'He used to drag us all to the shooting range . . . showing off . . . and Fulvio . . .'

So had Silvana really seen a man, as she'd half claimed, but was scared of admitting who? What if she'd seen it all? That 'confession' of hers, that she'd been buying shoes instead of being here to help her sister—wasn't it a bit early in the morning for that sort of shop? Well, that was easy enough to check and, in any case, once they had Paoletti under lock and key, perhaps they'd all find the courage to tell the truth.

'Come in the afternoon. He'll be out. I heard him on the phone.'

She'd certainly have plenty to say.

'It's all down to him.' Yes, but he was never on the scene.

'Where is Piero?'

Every time he'd spoken to her, she had asked

214

him that.

'*Where is Piero?*'

The tower stood empty of its prisoner, looming in the night. The marshal hadn't liked this place the first time he was here, and he didn't like it now.

What had happened here had happened in broad daylight. He was going home to sleep, and he would be back before any of them were awake.

As it happened, other things intervened and he wasn't.

Eleven

'I'm sorry to hear that, Guarnaccia. I know how much hung on it.' The captain's voice on the other end of the line was very sympathetic.

'Yes. It doesn't matter. His wife knows where he's going this afternoon. She overheard the telephone call we picked up.'

The newly assigned prosecutor had opened a file on The Emperor, and the phone was tapped. Paoletti would be there later in the day to 'audition' a new batch of girls. They might find nothing illegal on paper there or at the staffing agency, but domestic workers auditioning as pole dancers would warrant an explanation. So would the hotel. And those two children couldn't be explained away, even by Paoletti.

'You should be with us. If it hadn't been for you—'

'No, no. You don't need me. I'll go back up to Paoletti's place. Just in case . . .'

'In case?'

'I should go back there. Once I know you've got the girls and the children out . . . his wife will tell me everything I need to know. Do you think you'll get enough evidence on De Vita?'

'I'm sure of it. That retired marshal you found is a mine of information.'

'Nesti found him.'

'Apparently there was a complaint years ago about a blackmail scam involving the hotel. A man starting up an affair with the wife of a well-to-do citizen, taking her to the hotel and then someone sending photographs and threatening to tell the husband. Naturally, the boyfriend claimed he was being blackmailed too. Presumably that developed into the current blackmailing business with De Vita attracting customers by talking up the hotel. And, again, should they ever suspect him, he'd always claim he was being blackmailed too.'

'And so he would have been, if necessary.'

'That first woman who came for help claimed that there were at least two others, taken in by this same man, who didn't dare speak up. She'd found that out for herself. Some years have gone by, but she should be able to identify De Vita.'

'But not Paoletti. The invisible puppeteer as always.'

'We'll get him.'

The marshal, looking at the report lying in front of him, said, 'I don't know . . .'

'Guarnaccia, I understand that you feel he's slipped through your fingers; but, in any case, you know he didn't kill his daughter, that he was in hospital. You'll get to the bottom of it—besides, something will probably come out regarding the murder once we have these people in custody. The answer might still be outside the family.'

'Yes. I expect you're right. But this report means I'm wrong about it all, about him.'

'You can't argue with the science, Guarnaccia.'

'No. No, of course not.'

After he rang off, he read through the report again.

The DNA test showed that Piero Paoletti was the child of Daniela Paoletti and a person unknown, who was no relation to her.

'Even so . . .'

His big fingers tapped with a slow rhythm on the paper. He had wanted to be back up at Paoletti's place early, but the new prosecutor had asked to see him first thing, and once again he had reminded himself that Daniela was dead. The other, living victims must come first. When he arrived back at his office, this report had been on his desk.

Piero . . .

Was this concentrated concern for the child something Paoletti's drunken wife had transmitted to him?

'Where is Piero?'

It was almost eleven thirty. Paoletti was expected home at midday. The marshal would have liked to go to the hospital himself, a thing the prosecutor had prevented before. He wanted details as to Paoletti's health, he wanted his clinical notes. After all, he had discharged himself the other day and arrived home in a taxi. He wasn't that sick.

But he couldn't. Not yet, not until after the arrests.

A big operation had been mounted. They would

move in on the club, the hotel, and even the staffing agency here in the city at the same moment. There were witnesses: himself, Nesti, Piazza, Piazza's predecessor, the widower, the blackmailed wife. It couldn't go wrong. How could it go wrong?

No matter how hard he tried to convince himself otherwise, he couldn't shake his conviction that Paoletti would escape them.

And what was worse, in a way, was that even with the DNA report staring him the face, he couldn't or wouldn't accept that Paoletti wasn't the child's father.

He thought of sending Nesti to the hospital but, apart from the fact that he wouldn't be at his desk yet, Nesti couldn't obtain the clinical notes. Knowing Nesti, though, he'd get something. He'd have some nurse he could wind round his finger. But what use was that?

Besides, all Nesti's energies would be concentrated on the big scoop to come later; and he certainly deserved his moment.

Since there was nothing else useful he could do, he called for his driver and got ready to leave. He had no idea of bearding the lion in his den. He was just going to be there.

The lion had arrived before him.

The two carabinieri on duty informed him, 'He's been here about twenty minutes.'

'He arrived in a taxi and kind of nodded to us before he went in, as if we were on his staff. You know what I mean?'

'Yes. And that's how you should play it, too. We're here to protect his family.'

'Oh, and Marshal, two of the builders were

218

looking for you earlier.'

'What did they want?'

'Wouldn't say. Just said they had to speak to you.'

'All right.' He left his driver to move the car to a shady spot and went around the house to the right. There was no sound of any work going on. They would still be on their break. He found them in the old stables. They had set up house and a workshop for themselves in one of the boxes there. Their trowels hung on a length of thick string against the back wall, a stone manger held their bags and belongings, and the remains of their meal stood on an old wooden table they'd recouped from somewhere. They were all sitting on upturned buckets except for Cristiano who, with four buckets and two planks, had constructed a bed rather narrower than himself and was lying neatly disposed on his back, snoring. The men who were awake started to get up, but the marshal signed to them to stay as they were.

'Who was it wanted to talk to me?'

They all looked at the sleeping Cristiano, but it was the thin young man who'd been so upset over unpaid wages who got up and spoke.

'Cristiano . . .' But he didn't wake him. It was clear that Cristiano's afternoon nap was something of a sacred ritual. Nobody was going to wake him. The young workman who was on his feet pulled a bit of paper out of his pocket and offered it to the marshal.

'What's this?' It was just a dusty bit of paper. It was carefully folded, and there were two banknotes inside it.

'Ah. You've been paid.'

219

'Thank you.' The workman tried to indicate his gratitude by nodding and pointing at the money. 'Thank you.' He looked down at the sleeping Cristiano and again at the marshal, frowning.

'No, don't wake him. Good luck.' He withdrew from their little world thinking, as he went through the archway and approached the rear façade of the house where eyes had once watched him from behind those low grills, how within the space of a few hours he had uncovered two quite separate hidden worlds in this place. Well, it was also true that without the prosecutor's determined hijacking of the inquiry, he'd have discovered them on day one, along with a lot of other things. No use crying over spilt milk. He just had to make up for lost time. He walked on until he came to the pool, and decided to go up to the crime scene. Step by step, he had to go back over everything he'd seen and heard. Step by step. A lot of steps . . . He climbed the steep staircase, his hand on the cool smooth stone of the broad banister. As to where the prosecutor had been before getting himself here on the morning of the murder, the marshal felt pretty sure. He'd gone first to the hospital to confer—or to get his instructions . . . or . . . ?

He paused on the first floor, but only for breath, continuing up to the second-floor landing where he had stood that morning with the prosecutor, watching the carabiniere with the video camera filming the shells circled with chalk marks, the sloppy trail through the drawing room to the bedroom, the body, the white bedspread sprayed with red, broken glass. Running the memory back, then forward again, he paused every now and again to examine a detail. How different the same things looked now—and yet he had no key to some of the images: and they were the ones that, perhaps just because they were unexplained, kept returning. The shattered glass around the body on the rug, for instance. It had been important, of course, because it had explained—once they found the bullet—the extra shell. But that wasn't what kept coming back. What was in his head was an image he'd put together himself, rather than seen, though it had certainly existed. The body in a white bathrobe, red entrails spilling on the rug, and the ten-year-old Daniela with a bullet hole through her white communion dress.

'I thought we could play happy families.'

Had it started when the poor little girl was only ten? So thin, and he remembered such dark shadows under her eyes in the photograph.

And Paoletti in the hospital—another image he'd created but never seen. Another white image, a white hospital bed. Appropriate, anyway. Paoletti, the whited sepulchre.

What about the prosecutor? De Vita, for all his habitual arrogance, hadn't really been so sure of himself that day. Even if he had been to the hospital first, there was a lot of stuff he couldn't have known, unexpected stuff like Signora Donati across the road, his own presence rather than an emergency response car.

'What are the family members saying?'

That, too, an unknown quantity. What might the childish, hysterically weeping Silvana not have come out with?

'You think she's telling the truth?' His answer now, with hindsight, would be No.

'And the mother?'

221

He believed her, all right; who wouldn't? Which was why he'd been kept away from her.

He'd shown no interest in the doctor's findings. Other things on his mind. He'd tossed the idea of a robbery into the mix. Perhaps he wasn't such a Machiavelli, after all. Hiding plenty, yes, but otherwise groping in the dark. The captain was an intelligent man, and he'd warned against assuming that De Vita knew anything about the murder itself when he was only trying to deflect attention from his own crimes.

'Hmph.' The marshal opened the window and shutters behind the sofa. 'A bit more light . . . And besides, am I supposed to think this murder happened on his watch by coincidence? No, no . . .'

He remembered quite clearly the moment when, after gazing for a long time at the technicians working in this room, his thoughts still elsewhere, the prosecutor had decided that this slow and rather dimwitted marshal might be just what would suit him. Clapping him on the back and flashing those brilliant teeth at him . . .

'The blank incomprehension of the man!'

'You can't argue with the science, Guarnaccia.'

The marshal was unmoved. He remained convinced that the child was Paoletti's and that Paoletti, one way or another, was responsible for Daniela's death.

In the afternoon, the marshal and his driver watched from his car as Silvana left in the Mini to fetch Piero home from summer school. She returned with the child after forty minutes. Very soon afterwards they heard splashing and the child's shouts from the pool. The marshal got out and walked around the house to the right to take a

222

look at the scene from a distance. Paoletti was there in a deck chair in swimming trunks. The newspaper he was reading covered his belly. A pad was wrapped around one of his arms, measuring his blood pressure over twenty-four hours of activity. The little boy was splashing with his legs as Silvana pulled him along by his arms. Frida was serving drinks in tall glasses. She wore a bathing suit, too, so she must be allowed to swim in the pool, which surprised the marshal. Or was that how he got away with so much, doling out just enough little favours here and there to keep his victims psychologically as well as physically enslaved?

He was standing near the low curved grills along the base of the building. He saw her clearly this time, and she knew it. She was watching what he was watching. She couldn't have had a good view but, no doubt, she was listening too. She retreated, and so did he. Back at the car, the young carabiniere asked again, 'What's happening?'

It reminded him of the boys when they were small and bored by long car journeys.

Dad, when will we be there?

At least the two carabinieri in the squad car had each other to chat to.

He made an effort and told the lad about The Emperor and his visit there with Nesti.

'*How* much?'

'Sixty euros.'

'For ten minutes?'

'Ten minutes of nothing much. With an oven timer to tell you when.'

'I've never been to a night club.'

'No, well, you haven't missed much.'

'Is he dangerous, Paoletti?'

'Yes.'

'Did he kill his daughter?'

'I don't know.'

'But you don't think anything will happen? Here, I mean?'

'Nothing will happen until the raid at seven.'

'No . . . but you're staying here anyway, right?'

'That's right.'

What was it he used to say to his boys? Whoever is the first to see the sea . . .

And he'd invent some prize or other—or, more likely, that would have been left to Teresa.

'Go over to the squad car and check whether anything's come in over the radio.'

The carabiniere went across and leaned towards the passenger-side window. He talked to the others for a while and then, just as he was straightening up, he spun round on the gravel and ran towards the tower. The other two got out of the car and ran after him. The marshal, following, heard splashes and a woman screaming and screaming.

When they turned the corner of the tower, Frida was climbing out of the pool with Piero limp in her arms; Silvana was in the water screaming. At a distance, the marshal saw the thin young builder running towards the pool with big Cristiano behind him. They stopped when they saw all the uniforms. But the one thing that made the marshal's heart sink was an empty deck chair. Paoletti was gone.

One of the carabinieri took the child, lay him on the grass, and started trying to revive him. After what seemed an age, he began to choke and then to cry, but his cries were drowned out by Silvana's screams. The marshal went closer to the edge of the pool and helped her out. Her screams increased in volume.

'Stop it! He's all right. Put your robe on.' She was no doubt oblivious of being half naked in front of so many strangers, but the marshal was very conscious of the dark hair streaming over her brown breasts which, combined with her screams, could be a recipe for trouble. She obeyed him. Frida, in a too-large bathing suit, her thin white body burned red and peeling on the shoulders, was silent. She looked terrified and she avoided the marshal's eyes. He caught her looking beyond the pool at the two builders, who had retreated a few steps but were still there watching.

Paoletti reappeared, hurrying from the direction of the main house and he was dressed—or almost dressed. He was rolling his shirtsleeve down over the blood-pressure pad. His face was red and he began shouting—at the carabinieri, at Silvana, who was coming out of the tower wearing a bathrobe, and at Frida, especially at Frida.

The marshal walked away. As he passed the rear central doors of the house, he saw that they were standing open. The mother was there. She was dressed, but she stayed in the shadows. He stopped.

'Is he all right?'

'He's all right.'

'You're not leaving?'

'No.'

He walked on until he reached the two builders, who were waiting for him.

'There was something you wanted to say to me, wasn't there? It wasn't just the money.'

The younger man looked at him, then at Cristiano, who spoke for him.

'I told him he should have woken me. Is the kiddie all right?'

'For now. What was it you wanted to tell me?'

'It was him saw it, not me. Working on the roof of the stables.'

'What did he see?'

'Like today. He heard all this screaming, and the kiddie was in the water drowning. The dark girl did all the screaming—she's the owner's daughter and she's always screaming. She was in the water, but she did nothing except panic. It was the blonde girl got the kiddie out, same as now.'

'Was the owner there? Did you see him?'

Cristiano spoke to the other builder, who shook his head as he replied.

'No. He says there was nobody else there.'

'Did he see the child fall in? What is he saying?'

'He says no. Only, with that murder, we're a bit nervous, you know? He says it's happened twice when he's been on the roof.'

'Twice before today? Three times altogether?'

The younger man listened to Cristiano and nodded, his blue eyes earnest. He would have spoken volumes, had he been able.

Cristiano said, 'I hope we did right to tell you.'

'Yes, you did right—and don't worry. I'm hoping this will all be over by tomorrow. He did pay you, your boss?'

'Yes, he did, thanks to you. You must have scared him.'

'Mmph. Don't be surprised, though, if this job falls through.'

When he walked back to his car, the Mercedes

had gone. His driver, looking up at him, seemed happier now that something had happened. That was unkind. He was young and active and just wanted to be doing something.

'What do you think, Marshal?'

'What about?'

'Didn't you hear Paoletti shouting at the blonde girl? Accusing her? She was scared to death, and by the end she was in tears. She said all she'd done was go inside for a minute to put some cream on. Her shoulders were burning, she said—and they were, too. She's as white as a sheet. She's foreign—did you hear how she talked?'

'Polish. She's Polish.' He didn't get in the car. He remembered the sharp ironic glance when he'd said he had men positioned here. And yet her face just now . . .

You're not leaving?'

He'd have kept hold of that child himself, but he couldn't take any risks until Paoletti was safely handcuffed. And what was worse, he didn't understand the nature of the danger posed by Paoletti's absence, only that it existed. He remembered the mother's words about keeping people out and keeping them in. Which of the two were the four of them doing out here? The marshal wasn't sure, but he wasn't leaving. A telephone call from De Vita didn't help.

'Don't leave there, especially if, for any reason, Paoletti has to go out.'

Meaning Paoletti had already told him where he was going and didn't want to be followed.

'We'll be here.'

Still, the marshal didn't get into his car. He went back to the house and down to the kitchen. Frida

227

was giving the little boy something to eat at the big table. Danuta was washing a salad. He went up to her.

'Where is Silvana?'

'Getting dressed. We have to leave early.'

He went to the table and patted Piero's blond curls.

'You'll have to learn to swim.'

'I *can* swim! With my legs, and I'm going to learn to swim with my arms.'

'You're not frightened?'

'No!'

The only person in this family who wasn't, except Paoletti. Though, of course, the child was a male.

The marshal walked over to the mother's door and knocked. He could feel the shocked silence behind him. He didn't wait for an answer but walked in. She was on her feet. She'd heard him come down.

'You understand what happened out there?'

She hesitated and turned away from him. 'He's taken one child from me.'

'Then don't let him take another.' He looked at his watch. 'Signora, I don't want you to tell me anything you're afraid to tell me.'

'But you won't leave?'

'No, I won't leave, but I have to follow the prosecutor's instructions.' She knew he was lying, he could see that, but he couldn't tell her anything that a call from Paoletti or De Vita might frighten out of her.

'You won't say you were in here?'

'No, but do something for me. You're dressed and . . .'

'You can say it. I'm sober. Though it seems I

228

won't have to sit through supper—he's gone out, hasn't he?'

'Yes, but sit through supper anyway. Stay close to the child, just for a couple of hours. Please.'

'Where's Silvana?'

'Frida says she's dressing to go out. Just go in the kitchen like you always do in the evenings. Stay together.'

He went back to his car and waited until they saw Silvana and Danuta come out and get into the Mini. So, they were leaving early—something to do with the auditions, maybe? But something else was different, too. Silvana was dressed normally in a denim skirt, printed cotton shirt, brown leather sandals, but she was carrying a biggish holdall. What did that mean? They would be heading towards the station. Could she be running away? Something unexpected was going to happen, right now at the eleventh hour.

'Start your engine.'

As they turned and passed close to the squad car, he leaned out of the window.

'Make regular checks inside. Tell the signora I'll be coming back.'

'When?'

'I don't know.'

There was a bit more traffic, the roads were no longer deserted, but they soon had the black Mini in sight, going downhill towards the city.

'She's taking the ring road, Marshal. She's not going to the station.'

'Follow her.'

Five minutes later it was obvious where she was heading. He called the captain.

'I thought she might be running away, but she's

following her father.'

'Have you any ideas why?'

'No. It doesn't matter. She could somehow mess up the operation.'

'I doubt that. Give me the registration number of her car.'

He gave it and rang off. He'd been afraid all along that Paoletti might get away. It could go wrong. Silvana, hysterical, weeping, screaming, could make it go wrong somehow, whatever she was up to.

'She'll take the next exit. Keep your distance, I'll give you directions to the club. She mustn't see us.'

'We're going to be in on it, after all!'

'Not if she messes it up. Take the second on the left. Stop here.'

He called the captain, who was with the men heading for the hotel.

'What if she knows something, warns him?'

'She can't know anything. It'll be over in twenty minutes. Tell me where you're parked.'

There was nothing to do but wait and go in with them. At least the children were at the hotel, not here, so that even if Paoletti got away . . .

With all those uniforms outside, even the marshal began to believe they'd get him. At this hour, they'd found the carpark unattended, the foyer empty, the cash desk unlit. Loud thudding music came from behind the curtain, but the lighting, when the marshal took a discreet look, was just a couple of red spots, no disco spinnings and flashings.

Paoletti was there. He was in a big leather armchair facing the stage. The music was never interrupted, but he occasionally stabbed his finger towards one of the half-naked girls. 'You! No, you! Get off. Tell that one there to take that top off.'

The man the marshal thought was Mauro was sitting on the edge of the stage, wearing that same orange baseball cap, making notes on a clipboard and giving the girls instructions. Another man was taking photographs, and two more were deep in conversation, not even looking at the stage.

'And tell the one in the crappy blond wig to take it off and open her legs more when she goes down. She's got a good body, but she doesn't know how to move. No, no! Oh, for Christ's sake!'

A couple of men just on the other side of the curtain were sniggering as the girl who didn't know how to move started pulling her sequined knickers down.

'Like she's going to pee!'

'I *said* lose the wig!'

Someone touched the marshal's shoulder, and he stood back. The uniformed men moved in quickly and quietly. There was no fuss. Only the girls on the stage moved, reaching for something to cover themselves. Somebody shouted 'Switch that music off!'

The marshal went into the room, pushing past the uniforms, the groups of frightened girls, the handcuffed men. Paoletti was still there. He was still in his chair, but he was leaning forward to one side and his breathing was noisy.

Somebody said, 'I think he's ill.'

'Probably the shock when he saw us.'

Two carabinieri pulled him up so that his head fell back on the top of the armchair. His mouth was twisted and dribbling. Under the marshal's gaze, his eyes glazed over. He'd escaped.

Somebody screamed on the stage behind him. The marshal turned and saw the blond wig flung to the floor. The other girls were huddled together, pulling on such scanty clothes as they had. Only one remained in the centre, naked, screaming and screaming in desperation.

'You're not looking at me! You're still not looking at me!'

The marshal stepped onto the stage. She didn't see him. He might as well not have been there. She was screaming at Paoletti, but his darkened eyes saw nothing now. It wasn't the shock of the raid that had killed him.

'Daddy! Daddy, *look* at me!'

The marshal said, 'Cover her.'

She fought them, roaring and sobbing, but they managed to get her off the stage. There was nothing much to cover her with, so the marshal sat her in one of the alcoves under guard, still roaring, and went to find Danuta. She had been taken to the foyer and was standing there in jeans and T-shirt and rubber gloves, looking odd next to the half-naked girls. One or two were whimpering, but most were too frightened to make any noise.

'Do you know where Silvana's clothes are?'

'In the dressing room.'

'Bring them to me in there.'

232

Twelve

Somebody had let Nesti in. He was wandering up and down the long room, cigarette in the corner of his mouth, eyes half closed, looking pleased. Nobody had been allowed to leave, names and addresses were still being taken; but, perhaps because of the empty stage and the cold, dim lights that had been switched on instead of the red spots, the place did have the feeling of a cinema after the performance when the overblown magic images have vanished and the real world intrudes—even to the detail of a draught of night air coming in from the open doors.

The marshal had Silvana dressed and quiet, still in the alcove. There was something frightening about the way she could switch her raging tears off and change character on the instant and, if they were still sitting here in the middle of all this movement rather than talking in private, it was because the marshal had no intention of being alone with her, ever.

In her plaintive little girl's voice, she asked him, 'Why are they just leaving Daddy there? Why don't they get an ambulance?'

'They will get an ambulance, but he can't be touched until a doctor has examined him and pronounced him dead. It'll take time, I'm sorry. The ambulance would make no difference now. Turn away. Talk to me.'

'Talk to you? What about?'

'Yourself. You've had a very difficult life, by anybody's standards.'

'It was all right until she came.'

'She . . . ?' His first thought was Daniela, but she was two years older. 'Until who came?'

'Daniela. Why did he do that? Why? And Mummy never said a word. She just drank and drank and never said a word!'

'Excuse me, Marshal, one of the women—'

'Not now.' He held up a hand to stop the interruption without taking his eyes off Silvana.

'*I'm* his real daughter.'

'Yes. Of course.'

'You know? Did Mummy tell you?'

'No, no . . . not exactly. Did she talk to you about it?'

'They had to tell me when they brought Daniela home. I don't know who the father was, some man my mother was with before she met Daddy. She's not my father's daughter!'

'No.'

Of course not. You can't argue with science. The DNA test showed that Piero was the child of Daniela Paoletti and a person unknown who was no relation to her. Paoletti.

'How old were you when they brought her home? If they told you what was happening, you must have been old enough to understand.'

'I was eight.'

'So Daniela was ten. Do you know where she'd been all those years?'

She shrugged. 'Some orphanage. She was skinny and ugly and she never spoke. Mummy spoiled her and fussed over her and bought her presents. You'd think she was a princess. The ugly princess.'

'That must have been hard for you, after being the only child all those years. She was clever, too,

234

wasn't she? You told me once, I think, when you were telling me about her studying a lot and never talking to you, that she was like that when she was ten.'

'She always had to be top of the class. She wasn't all that clever. She only hid behind a book all the time because she was ugly.'

'But you were pretty and talented, weren't you? If you hadn't been ill . . . were you really ill, or did you give up? You said you spent a long time in hospital.'

'In a clinic. They sent me away. They shut me up in a clinic in Switzerland. They said I was mad. I'm not mad. They filled me with drugs, pills that made me sleepy all the time. That's what made me mad. They did that to me! And she stayed at home. The ugly princess stayed at home with Mummy and Daddy. Nobody wanted me any more, that's what it was!'

Somebody, perhaps trying to switch off the console inexpertly, set the thudding music off. It jangled the marshal's nerves, but then it stopped at once.

'Why isn't the ambulance coming? Daddy! He's not dead at all, you lied to me—Daddy! He's breathing. Listen!'

'It's all right. It's just the thing on his arm you can hear. It switches itself on every so often.'

It was true that it sounded like a groaning intake of breath, a hissing exhalation, another groan. It was finding nothing.

'Make it stop!'

'I can't. I can't touch anything until the doctor arrives. Don't look. Look at me. Tell me about you, not about Daniela. Do they believe you, now,

235

that you're not mad? Or do they still try to make you takc pills that you don't need?'

'They can't force me. I flush them away. Then I feel properly awake. I feel good.'

'I can imagine. But . . . even then . . . what's been going on with Daniela . . . little Piero . . . that sort of thing would upset you whether you were taking pills or not, I'm sure.'

'He gave that beautiful gold chain to her. All I got was an ordinary chain with a crucifix and a watch. She had a party for her whole class and a white velvet dress with tight, pointed sleeves that hooked on to her middle finger with a ring of real pearls. Mummy sewed them on. And a wreath of lily-of-the-valley made of green and white velvet.'

Big tears were spilling from her eyes, but she wasn't getting hysterical. He didn't stop her, only handed her his handkerchief.

'Marshal? We're about ready to move out . . .'

'Tell your commanding officer to leave me two men. I need some time—and let my driver know, will you?'

'Yes, of course. He's leaving two men anyway, because the doctor hasn't arrived yet. They'll be back there by the curtain—oh, and there's that girl who wanted you—not one of the dancers, she's—'

'Ah, yes.' He stood up to look. 'Stay here with her a moment, will you?'

'Where are you going? You're not leaving me? Don't leave me!'

'I won't leave you. Let me get rid of all these people so we can talk in peace.'

He went to Danuta, who was being held at the back of the room, white and anxious, looking for him.

236

'It's all right. I'll deal with her.'

'She said it was his orders, that she had to bring me here instead of to the train. It's not my fault!'

'It doesn't matter, Danuta. It's over. He's dead.'

But she was looking down the room at the body in the big chair.

'Look at me, Danuta. Don't be frightened. Has she done this before?'

'The last two auditions. He didn't see her the first time.'

'But the second time, he did?'

'She had a wig on that time, too, but he recognized her—what are they doing?'

The body was suddenly alight with swirling colours. Voices called out orders. It went dark. A white light came up slowly.

'He's moving! He's not dead, I saw him. He moved.'

'No, no. It was just the lights moving. They're trying to get some stronger light on the body for when the doctor arrives.'

'His arm moved.'

'No, no . . .' He turned to the two carabinieri. 'Keep her with you. I'll take her back to Florence with me.'

He went back and sat down with Silvana again.

She repeated in a toneless voice, 'Don't leave me on my own.'

'I won't leave.'

The big room was quiet now. In the centre, in front of the stage, Paoletti's body, slumped in the armchair, was brightly lit.

'Daddy . . .'

'Don't look there. Look at me. Tell me. How did you find out about this place?'

237

'From a girl who'd been sent to work as a cleaner. She came back to the office and asked me to find her another job because there was this incontinent old man and she couldn't stand it. She told me Daddy had turned her down for the club because her breasts were flaccid. Then I knew what the pretty girls I put on the list were for. They weren't being interviewed as receptionists and models, they were for here. I put the name of an ugly girl on the list and took her place.'

'So, you were the one who made the list. But didn't Mauro, the driver, recognize you?'

'Oh, no. I wore a wig and kept quiet. They can't speak Italian when they arrive. He pushed us into the back of a minivan without even looking at us.'

'I see. But your father was bound to recognize you.'

'Of course! Only, the first time he was called away and left the manager to audition. I wanted to sing, but they only wanted dancers. The next time I sang for Daddy.'

'The time he was taken ill?'

'Yes. I had red hair and false eyelashes. I thought he'd recognize me when I sang, though. I wanted to surprise him.'

'I'm sure you did.'

'But he just sat there!'

'Because he was ill.'

'Maybe. He was furious with me, but it wasn't my fault. My voice is trained for classical music. They were laughing at me. They were laughing this time too, but it was only because of the wig.'

'Yes, I think it was.'

'I have beautiful breasts. Not like Daniela. She was far too fat, even though when she was ten she

238

was far too skinny. Skinny and ugly.'

'Did you fight with Daniela?'

'How could I fight her? She was bigger than me.'

'Of course. Two years' difference is a lot. I bet you got your own back sometimes, though.'

She wiped her wet face on his handkerchief, but more tears spilled over.

'Only once.'

'How did you do it?'

'She had this pathetic rag doll that she brought with her when she came from the orphanage. She never let go of it, but I took it when she was asleep.'

'What did you do to it?'

'I drowned it. It was a stupid cheap thing and the colours ran so it had no face when Mummy got it out. It wasn't the big pool we have now. The one at the other house was smaller. Daddy taught me to swim in it.'

'I remember, you told me. Were you punished for what you did?'

'He beat me.'

'He didn't beat you yesterday when Piero almost drowned.'

'You were all there. Otherwise, he would have beaten Frida.'

'Frida? Why?'

'She's supposed to keep watch when Daddy's not there. It's only because I tease Piero. I pull him along and pull him along and then, at the deep end, I let go. And just when he thinks he's drowning, I pull him out. It's only my joke to make him learn to swim.'

'Is that how you were taught to swim?'

'No. Daddy never jokes. He gets in a rage if you

239

don't do things right.'

'What else did he teach you?'

'To shoot at the range. Daniela's no good at that, so he only takes me.'

'Something you do together, just the two of you. That's nice.'

'And sometimes with Fulvio as well. I want him to take me to a restaurant after, just the two of us, like he used to when I was small, before *she* came, but he never does. He always wants to get back to eat lunch with Daniela and Piero.'

'But you all ate supper together. And Fulvio too, sometimes? I expect you learned his schedule and knew when he was the prosecutor on duty.'

She didn't answer, only blew her nose, tears still rolling, trickling under her chin and down her neck. Her T-shirt was wet with them. She was crazy, the marshal thought, but not too crazy to plan carefully. She was her father's daughter. He doubted this would ever come to court, so he'd never have to prove it, but he reckoned she'd put the child in the car and then gone back up and shot her sister before driving to summer school. Fulvio on call, the bulldozer to cover the noise, and the man in his garden across the road as a witness to her panic and distress when she got back—only that morning, for once, it had been his wife.

'How old was Daniela when she moved into the tower, do you remember?'

'When she was eighteen.'

But, of course. All legal and above-board.

'And you were sixteen. You must have been very upset.'

'When we were small, he used to come in our

240

bedroom and play games with both of us, but then he said we were big enough to have our own rooms. Why did he have to do it? Why did he have to ruin my whole life? Why?'

'Shh . . . keep calm, now. Shh.' Her face was reddening, a warning sign. 'It's all over now. And they're both gone. You shot your sister and you made sure you completed the job.'

'I'm a good shot. Daddy said. Daniela was useless.'

'You're a very good shot. It was easy at the door, but you didn't let her get to the phone and you didn't waste a shot. People think you did. Even Fulvio says you did, because you hit the First Communion photo, but that's not true, is it?'

She smiled through her tears.

'Anyway, your father and your sister are both dead. It's over.'

'No, it's not. It'll never be over, ever, because of his will.'

The first stroke. It had to have been the first stroke. He'd known it and stupidly hadn't thought of a will.

'Tell me about the will.'

'He made it in the hospital. He told us he'd divided the children's inheritance equally between the three of us, me and Daniela and Piero! It should have been me, me most of all, as his real daughter, and less for Daniela! And Piero should only have inherited her share after his mother's death!'

'And now his mother is dead.'

'So he gets two thirds! It's not fair! More than half of it should have been mine. Daddy had no right. I was his real child, his only real child. What

241

about me? What about *me!*'

'I'm sure you'll be well provided for . . .'

'That's not the point!'

'No. I understand that you feel hurt. And I understand what your family situation must have made you suffer. The secrecy. The shame. It must have been very hard to live with—'

'But why? I was his real daughter, I was the pretty one, I could have given him a child. Why didn't he want me, me, *me?* Why bring *her* home?'

To play happy families . . .

The marshal heard the ambulance siren and then movement at the door.

She didn't protest when they took her away. She didn't look back at the body in the armchair, alone in the almost-empty room. She seemed pleased to be the centre of attention. The marshal followed and watched as they put her in the car. She looked up at him, dry-eyed.

'I could almost feel sorry—for Piero, I mean. He was always nice to me.'

*   *   *

'It's the first time I've had to solve a case and investigate it afterwards.'

'And let's hope,' said the captain, 'that it's the last.'

The September morning was sunny, the cloister cool. They stood aside to let the colonel's car in.

'Let me offer you a coffee.'

They stopped off at the bar before reaching the exit.

'Two coffees, please. A drop of something in it?'

'No, no thank you.'

242

'Two coffees! Captain. Marshal. Something to eat? Brioche? Toast?'

'Not for me. You have something, Guarnaccia.'

'No. I mustn't. No . . . my wife . . .'

'So, a conviction for manslaughter's no more than I expected, but I'm afraid when it goes up on appeal . . . those are pretty fancy lawyers, and it'll be the usual "Good families, bright boys, future careers ruined, started as a prank, no intention to harm." The sentences will be reduced. I'd be surprised if they served eighteen months.'

'And if the children hadn't been gypsy children?'

'If they hadn't been gypsy children, it wouldn't have happened.' The captain paid, and they stepped out into the cloister. 'I gather your case isn't going to trial.'

'No, no . . . settled out of court. She was diagnosed years ago, so there was no question. The Beretta .22 was her own, did I tell you? Present from Daddy, she said. They found it in her room in all that chaos. Wigs, erotic outfits, and hundreds of photos of the two of them. And a diary. She stalked her father, everywhere he went. She's in a clinic up north, but the problems will start when she gets out and stops taking her medication.'

'Yes. Of course, now that the father and sister are gone, she might quieten down.'

'They say not. It's medication or nothing.'

'The things people do to their children.'

'I don't know.'

'But you said yourself, the father was monstrous.'

'Oh, yes. I was afraid of him, I don't mind telling you, but I've long ago lost my taste for blaming people. His daughter's like him. Whatever fancy

243

name they give it, she's crazy and dangerous like her father. She just wasn't as good at it. It's her mother we need to worry about. Like her daughter, Daniela. The born victims. Well, the main thing is that we're rid of De Vita.'

'But you'd have liked to get Paoletti.'

'No. It's better the way it is. Safer for everybody.'

'Your driver . . . ?'

'I sent him back. I'll walk over. One or two calls to make on the way, and there's never anywhere to stop. You didn't say if there was any news about the two children from the hotel.'

'The bureaucratic nightmare? Nothing new. I'm afraid it could go on for years. They're safe and happy out in the country where the prosecutor placed them, as you said they would be, but if they're to stay here they need documents and even though the sisters are orphans, they do have living relatives in Russia.'

'Who sold them.'

'Yes. The older one would be up to testifying about that. The important thing is not to have it blown up into a diplomatic incident. That would be the worst possible outcome. They'd be sent back. Better to go slowly and keep a low profile.'

'You mean keep Nesti off the case, I suppose. But if it hadn't been for him . . . However, I'll do my best.'

The guard saluted and the captain turned back.

The marshal walked upriver. He'd given up asking about Cristina. She hadn't been there when the captain's men raided the hotel. The other dancers from the club hadn't seen her for days. She hadn't got in touch with Maddalena. Of course, she could be prancing around half-dressed

244

on television under some other name. The marshal wasn't sure he would recognize her if he saw her. They were all so pretty, he couldn't tell one from another.

There was another woman he didn't recognize in the waiting room when he got back. He was walking through to his office with no more than a brief nod of greeting.

'Marshal?'

He stopped. 'Oh, Signora! And Piero! Come in, come in.'

'I hope I'm not disturbing you . . .'

'No, no . . . have a seat.' He hung up his hat and slipped his dark glasses into his top pocket. 'So, Piero! What have you been up to?'

'I've got new sneakers. Look.' He ran up and down the small room, making coloured lights flash on his heels.

'Good Heavens. I wonder if I could get a pair of those.'

'You can. They've got loads. You have to cross at the traffic lights and there's a big shop and the lady's got a Band-Aid on her arm, there, right near her elbow. I've got a Band-Aid too, but it's on my foot, so you can't see it.'

'Ah. And how do you like your new house?'

'I don't like it, because there's no swimming pool.'

'I see. Well, you can still go swimming. There are plenty of pools to go to.'

'I know, but Nana never takes me. Is that your hat hanging up?'

'You know it is, you saw me put it there. Do you want to wear it? Sit down there.'

Piero sat very still, keeping the hat balanced.

245

'I just wanted to let you know that I've sold the house and that I'm grateful to you for advising me to get out right away rather than waiting. I feel so much better.'

'You look wonderful.'

'It's just . . . Marshal, there's a lot of money. The lawyers have explained that there won't be a trial, that death extinguishes the crime. He got away with it to the last, didn't he?'

'Yes.'

'But all that money . . .'

'I understand what you mean. But you have Piero to think of, and there'll be a lot of expense in your life.'

They were both reluctant to name Silvana, but she was in both their minds.

'I'll never put Piero at risk again. I know I should have—Marshal, I'd lost one daughter. You do understand?'

'Yes. I understand.'

Silvana was in a clinic for a mandatory two years, but she would surely discharge herself after that and stop taking her medication. A problem without end.

'You're going to need money, and help, too.'

'Yes. I know you're right, and Frida's staying with me. Danuta's met somebody, so . . . But so much money and so much damage.'

'You suffered damage too, Signora.'

'Oh, my poor Daniela.'

'Why did he do what he did? No. I don't mean what you think. I mean how come he let you bring her home?'

'He didn't let me. That's not how it was. He insisted. It was because of Silvana. He put me

246

through a couple of abortions and then decided a man should have children. A respectable family. He wanted a son, of course, but then when Silvana came along she worshipped the ground he walked on. He loved that. He owned her and she adored him. He used to choose her dresses. And since I couldn't have any more, he decided to bring Daniela home.'

'He knew where she was?'

'Oh, yes. He'd promised the priest who married us that he'd adopt her. Then he didn't, until she was ten. You know, in spite of everything, he had a way of convincing you . . . he was so strong, and he could suddenly turn all this power and warmth on you and you'd feel so good after being so frightened.

'I never go to sleep at night without crying for her—not for her death, but for her life, for all those years of being abandoned. I should have found a way, I could have found a way, but I was scared and I wanted to be free—and look how I ended up. I wouldn't have ended up in *his* hands if I'd tried to keep my baby and, besides . . .'

'You loved the father, Daniele. I understand. But no, Signora. Don't torment yourself. You were very young and you were alone.'

'And you're very kind. But I've been a coward all my life, and now I'm rich. It doesn't make any sense.'

'No.'

'What happened to all those girls that he . . . ?'

'Some of them are still with Don Antonino. There's an amnesty coming up. He'll help them get papers and jobs. If you want to do something useful in memory of Daniela, instead of tormenting yourself, give Don Antonino some money. Goodness knows, he needs it.'

Her face lit up. It was still difficult to recognize her, so much slimmer, younger-looking and well-dressed.

'I was sure you'd help me.'

'You'll be all right. You have a new life now, a fresh start. And this little boy to love.'

'You're a good man. If there's ever anything I can do for you, just say the word.'

'Well'—Piero was stamping to the door, heels flashing—'you could rescue my hat.'

* * *

'So, what did you think of it?'

'Better than the last one. There was so much more light.'

'Well, but Salva, it was on the top floor so of course there was more light, and it was a beautiful autumn day too. But you have to think about all those stairs. There's no space for an elevator, you know. It's the same in all these old Florentine buildings. The stairwells are so tiny, except in the really grand buildings. Think of carrying shopping up there, think of carrying cases of mineral water.'

'But you keep saying it's only an investment. We're not going to live there, we're just trying to get a foot on the housing ladder. That's what you said.'

'Even so, a hundred and ten steps . . .'

'All right.'

'Perhaps we should look at something new, a bit further out of the centre.'

'All right.'

'Or in a bigger building where there's an elevator.'

'All right.'

'Salva! For goodness' sake stop saying All right. It's no help at all if you don't give me your opinion. You're not *still* brooding on that Tyrant of Syracuse thing, are you?'

'No.'

'Well, what, then?'

'I want to watch the news. Something I need to see.'

It was only the local news, and it was squeezed between a protest about the new tramway and the transfer of a Fiorentina player.

The body, what was left of it, had been found by mushroom gatherers. It was fully clothed. A handbag was recovered in a nearby stream. It contained no documents that could identify the woman, judged to be around eighteen to twenty years old, but it did contain a number of carefully posed photographs. One came up on the screen. Dark, pretty curls, a smiling red mouth, and sad, painted eyes. Cristina had made it. She was on television.

MCSM